Heathcliff Redux

A Novella and Stories

Also by Lily Tuck

Sisters

The Double Life of Liliane

The House at Belle Fontaine

I Married You for Happiness

Woman of Rome: A Life of Elsa Morante

The News from Paraguay

Limbo and Other Places I Have Lived

Siam or the Woman Who Shot a Man

The Woman Who Walked on Water

Interviewing Matisse or the Woman Who Died Standing Up

Heathcliff Redux
A Novella and Stories

Lily Tuck

Atlantic Monthly Press
New York

FIRST EDITION

Published simultaneously in Canada
Printed in the United States of America

First Grove Atlantic hardcover edition: February 2020

This book was designed by Norman E. Tuttle of Alpha Design & Composition. This book is set in 13.5-point Centaur MT by Alpha Design & Composition of Pittsfield, NH.

Library of Congress Cataloging-in-Publication data is available for this title.

ISBN 978-0-8021-4759-2
eISBN 978-0-8021-4760-8

Atlantic Monthly Press
an imprint of Grove Atlantic
154 West 14th Street
New York, NY 10011

Distributed by Publishers Group West

groveatlantic.com

20 21 22 23 10 9 8 7 6 5 4 3 2 1

Contents

Heathcliff Redux   5

Labyrinth Two   163

The Dead Swan   185

Carl Schurz Park   195

A Natural State   203

Acknowledgments   215

Heathcliff Redux

Whether it is right or advisable to create beings like Heathcliff, I do not know: I scarcely think it is. But this I know: the writer who possesses the creative gift owns something of which he is not always master—something that, at times, strangely wills and works for itself.

—Charlotte Brontë

OF COURSE I had read *Wuthering Heights*. I read it years ago in high school, but, in my late twenties, I decided to read it again. I also had seen the movie version with Merle Oberon and Laurence Olivier, and I particularly remember the scene, early on in the film, that presages the characters' tragic misconceptions: Catherine tells Heathcliff how she thinks he is a prince in disguise and that his father must have been the emperor of China and his mother an Indian queen.

I first saw Cliff—everyone called him that—in April, at a steeplechase race. Charlie, my husband, and I and Meryl and Frank, our neighbors, had driven over there together. The back of our truck was loaded with hampers filled with food, wine, and bottles of bourbon. The race was a popular annual event, attended by people (mostly gentry) from all over the county. Originally a single race with gentlemen riders, the event had grown to include several races and the riders were no longer necessarily gentlemen. The course was four miles long and the fences were tall and timber. Charlie and I were both riders and we owned a couple of Thoroughbred hunters. We knew a lot of the horse people at the race—after all, we had been going there for several years—and before one of the races, Charlie and I walked over to the paddock where the horses and their riders were getting ready, tightening girths, adjusting stirrups, and mounting their horses, and it was there that I first saw—no, stared at—Cliff. My husband saw him, too, because he made some comment—I don't remember exactly what he said. Something like "Jeez, look at how that guy gets on his horse." That was it exactly. Instead of getting "a leg up" the way most of the riders did, Cliff just jumped into the saddle. Like he was a Cossack or something. A leap, I would call it. And his horse was at least sixteen hands tall. It was impressive. I remember how it looked to this day—to my dying day, probably.

Charlie and I lived on a four-hundred-acre farm in Albemarle County, Virginia—one of the richest counties in the country. Charlie had grown up on the farm and now he managed it for his parents, who had retired to Florida. Besides the horses, he raised beef cattle. Black Angus. For a while he kept a bull, but then artificial insemination became popular and more convenient. It was also cheaper and Charlie got rid of the bull. His name was Hannibal. I was glad, because even if he was kept separate in a field, I was afraid of him.

During the steeplechase race, a big bay gelding named Patrick's Dream fell after clearing a jump and broke his front leg—both front legs, someone later told Charlie—and they had to put him down. Luckily I didn't see that. I just saw the truck dragging the harness go out onto the field. Always an upsetting sight. Briefly I wondered whether it was the leaper's horse who had broken his legs but it wasn't. The leaper had been riding a gray horse. I have always been partial to gray horses.

Native Dancer, who won the Preakness and the Belmont, was a gray. He just missed winning the Kentucky Derby and getting the Triple Crown (Eric Guerin, his jockey, was blamed for taking him all over the track except the ladies' room), but he was named U.S. Champion Three-Year-Old Colt in 1953 and U.S. Horse of the Year in 1954.

From our house, I could see the Blue Ridge Mountains in the distance. (The reason the mountains appear blue and hazy, I have been told, is on account of the isoprene released from the trees.) Besides the beef cattle, we grew corn to feed them. In the summer, Charlie and a couple of hired farmhands harvested the corn. Some days the temperature reached 100 degrees, and the humidity made the heat feel a lot worse. Always, in the air, there was the threat of rain or, worse, of a thunderstorm. (One summer, it hailed—hail as big as grapefruits—breaking car windshields and most of the storefront windows in town.) At midday, I drove the truck down to the field bringing the men cold lemonade and ham sandwiches. I usually wore shorts and I can still recall how my legs stuck uncomfortably to the plastic seat. My hands, too, were sweaty, which made it difficult to hold the wheel and steer.

"How's it going?" I asked.

"Hot as hell," Charlie would answer.

"Next time, bring me a beer," he also said.

The hired hands took the sandwiches and the lemonade without saying a word and without looking at me.

Both of them were black.

"I think it's going to rain," I said, looking up at the sky and trying to engage.

"You better get back in the truck and go home," Charlie said.

The year was 1963, and the early '60s was still a relatively innocent time—innocent, at least, for middle-class people like Charlie and me. We did not do drugs, we did not get divorced, and we did not have abortions or extramarital love affairs, or, if we did, we did not talk about them.

As yet, Martin Luther King Jr. had not been shot and killed. Nor had anyone whom I knew or had heard of.

The next time I saw Cliff was at the Keswick Hunt Club Ball. (I normally tried to avoid those events. Not only did I have to get dressed up, but I had to get a babysitter. Also, Charlie tended to drink too much, and I'd have to drive the truck home at God knows what hour in the morning.) Cliff was dancing cheek to cheek with a woman I knew slightly. Her name was Sally. When Sally saw me looking at her and Cliff, she waved at me with the hand that was resting on Cliff's shoulder and I waved back.

Sally was a rich widow in her late forties. She owned a grand historic house that had once been a plantation and was often compared to Monticello. The house was open to the public a few times a year to benefit a local charity and, several times, it had been written up and photographed in fashion magazines. Sally's husband, who died the year before in a car accident (his car overturned in a drainage ditch at night, and he was pinned inside it and not found until the next morning, when it was too late), had been at least fifteen years older than Sally, and he had made his fortune with some paper products—I've forgotten what they were exactly. Packaging, I think. They did not have children. Sally wasn't beautiful, but she was attractive and had a good, trim figure. She was an excellent sportswoman—she rode (she was a whipper-in at the local hunt), was a good shot, played golf and tennis, and I don't know what else. She was also on a bunch of committees—at the library in town, a small liberal arts college in Lynchburg, the hospital—because she gave to them generously. I couldn't fault her for that. In fact, I couldn't fault her for anything—not even for dancing with Cliff.

"Banish him from your thoughts, miss . . . He's a bird of bad omen; no mate for you," Nelly, both narrator and housekeeper in *Wuthering Heights*, warns.*

---

* Emily Brontë, *Wuthering Heights* (London: Penguin Books, 2003), p. 103.

Hannibal, our bull, was not an Angus but a Charolais. The Charolais is one of the top meat-producing breeds, and Charlie had bought him with the hope of improving our herd. The Charolais comes from Charolles, France, and was imported to Mexico in 1930. Hannibal, according to an article I read, could trace his lineage back to two Mexican bulls called Neptune and Ortolan.

(Ortolan? An ortolan is a tiny bird, the size of my thumb, that weighs less than an ounce. It is a French delicacy prepared by first throwing the bird into a vat of Armagnac to both marinate and drown it, then cooking it for eight minutes and serving it whole. Traditionally, diners eat ortolans—heads, bones, and all—with a napkin thrown over their heads.)

"What does 'Cliff' stand for?" I asked, when, at last, I met him. "'Clifford'?"

"Something like that," he answered, smiling.

It was at a cocktail party celebrating Sally's forty-ninth birthday; I was drinking my second glass of wine and wearing a sleeveless white dress.

"Or does it stand for 'Heathcliff'?" I persisted. "You know, Heathcliff in *Wuthering Heights*."

"Heathcliff? Who's that?" Cliff asked, still smiling.

"You've never read *Wuthering Heights*?" Right away, I regretted saying that. I was afraid of sounding superior and assuming he did not read books and was not, like me, educated. Since he did not answer, I said lamely, "It's one of my favorite novels. I'm rereading it now."

"Is that so?" Cliff said.

Nervous, I nodded, and in spite of feeling myself start to blush, I went on. "Heathcliff is the hero, or, more accurately, the antihero, who—"

"Sounds interesting," Cliff interrupted me softly. "Maybe I should read it. And you know something? You are a pretty woman."

Maybe he had not read *Wuthering Heights* and maybe he was not educated, but he was very handsome. There was no getting around that.

In bed that night, I asked Charlie if he knew who Heathcliff was.

"Yeah, of course. Why are you asking me? He's the character in the novel—what's it called—the novel with the crazy wife in the attic."

"Do you mean *Jane Eyre*?"

"Yes, *Jane Eyre.*"

"You don't mean Mr. Rochester?" I said.

"What is this? An exam?" Charlie asked, sitting up.

"You must mean *Wuthering Heights* by Emily Brontë," I said.

"Okay, okay. I meant the guy in *Wuthering Heights*," Charlie said, lying down again and turning over and away from me in bed.

"Go to sleep," he also said.

Hindley had asked for a fiddle, Cathy for a new whip, but when their father, Mr. Earnshaw, returned from Liverpool, he brought them Heathcliff.

And true, as I would learn later, Cliff never did read *Wuthering Heights.*

At the time—a time of unapologetic social-class labeling and bias—the good people of Albemarle County were divided into three groups: "town," "gown," and "county." We were "county," while Cliff was definitely "town."

Our neighbors, Meryl and Frank—actually, they lived across the road from us—did a number of things, including running the diaper service in town and boarding horses. They also had a lot of apple trees on their property. One time, when they let some of the horses out into a field where apples were lying rotting and fermenting on the ground, the horses ate them and got drunk. It was kind of funny to watch them staggering around and falling down, but it was pretty awful, too. Like the whole world had all of a sudden gotten unsteady. Meryl and Frank had several children, all of them girls.

Emily Brontë was also a poet:

> *No coward soul is mine*
> *No trembler in the world's storm-troubled sphere*
> *I see Heaven's glories shine*
> *And Faith shines equal arming me from Fear . . .**

---

* Emily Brontë, *The Complete Poems* (London: Penguin, 1992), p. 182.

At that cocktail party celebrating Sally's birthday, I learned that the gray horse Cliff had ridden in the race was hers. I should have guessed that. I also found out that he and Sally were sleeping together. I should have guessed that, too. Apparently, Cliff came in fourth in the race—not that I cared. But I did.

I care a lot about horses and about horsemanship. The way someone rides, I think, tells a lot about that person. For instance, Charlie is a good rider. He rides primarily from strength. I don't object to that as long as he does not abuse his strength. Charlie rides with his thighs while I ride with my ass. I ride from empathy. I try to second-guess what my horse will do and anticipate it. I don't wear spurs or use a whip. I've ridden almost all my life—at least since I was five years old. I feel good on a horse and the horse usually knows that.

The first horse I rode was a pony called Freddy. Like a lot of ponies, Freddy was mean. Because of a Napoleonic complex, or what? Freddy did his best to buck me off, or he would reach around and try to bite me while I was mounting him; a couple of times he would get down on his knees and start to roll, but I always managed to get off him in time. Funnily enough, none of that meanness bothered or deterred me. After Freddy, came Delia, a palomino mare who was gentle and kind and on whom I learned to jump. I had Delia for seven years—grooming and feeding her and mucking out her stall every day. I loved her dearly. Then one day while we were out riding, she shied a few times for no discernible reason; later, when I let her out in the field, she ran smack into the fence. She had contracted what is commonly referred to as moon blindness and officially known as equine recurrent uveitis, for which, unfortunately, there is no known cause or cure. I was heartbroken. My next horse was a tricky black colt named Balthazar—Balt for short. I had to train him—lunge him, get him used to the saddle, me on top of the saddle, the whole nine yards. I learned a lot.

"Too good-looking for his own good," the same person who said Cliff was having an affair with Sally told me. "He's reckless and he's an operator, he's cheating on his wife and I wouldn't trust him as far as I could throw him, he'd probably rob his own grandmother if he could, he's nothing but trouble, mark my words . . ."

"Heathcliff's enduring appeal is approximately that of Edmund, Iago, Richard III, the intermittent Macbeth: the villain who impresses by way of his energy, his cleverness, his peculiar sort of courage; and by his asides, inviting, as they do, the audience's or reader's collaboration in wickedness."*

---

* Joyce Carol Oates, "The Magnanimity of *Wuthering Heights*," *Critical Inquiry* 9, no. 2 (Dec. 1982): 435–49.

Meryl and Frank's oldest daughter, Carol, came over and babysat from time to time. She was fourteen, wore glasses, and always brought a book along with her—last time she came over she was reading *A Tale of Two Cities*. Not only did I approve, I thought she seemed reliable.

But she was shy and hard to talk to.

"Do you kids ride over at your place?" I asked her.

She shook her head.

"No? Why not? Your dad has a bunch of nice horses there."

Shrugging, she held her book up to her chest as if in defense. "I'm afraid of horses," she said.

"Oh, that's too bad," I said.

"The last time I rode, I fell off and broke my arm," Carol said.

"Did you get back on again?"

Carol shook her head. She looked as if she was about to cry.

"I fell off once and broke my collarbone—I was about your age, maybe a little older—and my dad made me get right back on the horse, although it hurt like crazy. I thought I was going to pass out," I told her.

Carol said nothing.

"How do you like *A Tale of Two Cities*?" I asked, to change the subject.

Lela, Bella, and Nelly—all bitches—were the names of our three dogs. Lela and Bella, the English springer spaniels, belonged to Charlie and he hunted birds with them—quail, pheasant, ducks, and doves. Nelly, a Norwich terrier, belonged to me. Nelly was eight years old and going a little deaf, and, like all terriers, she was stubborn and disobedient, and I adored her.

Keeper, Emily Brontë's dog, was fierce and unruly and obeyed only her. When Emily died at the age of thirty, "her devoted Keeper, whom she had treated with the sort of feeling usually reserved for human beings, walked in the short cortège of Charlotte, Anne, the servants and Mr. Brontë, behind the wooden coffin through the graveyard in the biting wind. He was taken into the church and the Brontës' own pew, where he sat quietly while the burial service was read. And for the next week he lay outside Emily's bedroom and howled."*

---

* Rebecca Fraser, *The Brontës: Charlotte Brontë and Her Family* (New York: Crown, 1988), pp. 318–19.

When we were first married, Charlie taught me how to shoot. He taught me how to shoot a pistol—his .44 Magnum with an ivory grip that he had bought from a dealer in Texas—and a shotgun. The shotgun was a double-barreled twelve-gauge, and the recoil hurt until I eventually got used to it and stopped anticipating it. Eventually, too, I got to be a pretty good shot and enjoyed going clay pigeon shooting with Charlie. I also surprised myself by how competitive I turned out to be and how determined I was to get a higher score than Charlie's. (In a standard clay pigeon round—or skeet shoot, as the sport is also known—each person gets to shoot at 25 "pigeons," and each "pigeon" is 3 points for a first barrel kill, 2 points for a second barrel kill, and, of course, 0 for a miss. The maximum per round is 75 points, and I usually scored in the mid- to high 60s.)

Charlie had taken a four-hour course with Lucky McDaniel, who taught "instinct shooting," and, for a while, Charlie could not stop talking about him. The premise was that you didn't aim, you just pointed at the target—the way, for instance, you point your finger or throw a baseball.

"He's taught thousands of people to shoot," Charlie told me. "From a six-year-old kid to an eighty-five-year-old grandmother."

"No kidding," I said, unconvinced.

"Lucky McDaniel also taught John Wayne to shoot."

But the time Charlie took me bird hunting, it was different. With my first shot, a dove fell out of the sky like a stone.

"Well done!" Charlie yelled. "See, what did I tell you? You didn't aim, right? You just shot at it."

Bella found the dove in the cornfield and brought it to Charlie.

"A clean shot," Charlie yelled again.

The dead dove was a mourning dove and monogamous, and I vowed then never again to shoot and kill anything.

Clay pigeon targets are made from a mixture of pitch and pulverized limestone rock and shaped like an upside-down soup dish. They are designed to both be tossed from traps at high speeds and break easily when hit by pellets from a shotgun.

The twins, Sam and Pete, were identical except for a small mole over Pete's right eyebrow. When they were babies, I painted one of Pete's fingernails bright red so that I could tell them apart easily. Now that they were nine years old, I could no longer do that. The twins were inseparable, private, smart, cute, and a little creepy.

Every weekday morning at 7:45, I drove them to the end of the driveway so that they could catch the school bus, and every afternoon at 4:10, I would drive down again and pick them up.

"How was school?" I asked.

"Fine," they answered together.

"What did you learn today?" I persevered.

"That the South won the Civil War." They both laughed. The sound of their laughter more like a cackle.

"That's not funny," I said.

Silence.

The South, the South. I hated the South. I hated the hypoc-
risy, the phony gentile manners, the accent, the racism. In all
the years—ten—that I had lived in Virginia, I had not met a
single black person. The only black persons I knew to speak
to—"hi there," "how're you doing," and "thanks"—were the
baggers in the supermarket, the boy who pumped gas into
the truck, a girl at a roadside stand who, in summer, sold
peaches, and the woman who came to the house once a week
to clean and whose name was Alice Washington.

Washington—for God's sake!

I am from New England originally, a small town in Massachusetts, famous for a pond.

I wondered where Cliff was from.

"It's a cuckoo's, sir—I know all about it; except where he was born, and who were his parents, and how he got his money at first," is how Nelly, the housekeeper in *Wuthering Heights*, describes Heathcliff.*

* Brontë, *Wuthering Heights*, p. 35.

A solitary bird known as a brood parasite, the cuckoo lays its eggs in another bird's nest, then leaves. When the baby cuckoo hatches—the cuckoo egg usually hatches first—he pushes all the other birds or eggs, as the case may be, out of the nest and takes all the food for himself from his surrogate parents.

I don't remember where I read this story. The story takes place during the Renaissance, in Florence. It seems that a certain countess, who lived in a beautiful palazzo, had her jewels stolen. Every day during one hot summer—the windows of the palazzo all left open—another ring, another bracelet and necklace, went missing from her dressing table in her bedroom. She accused her maid. The maid denied any knowledge of the missing jewels, but the maid was fired. More servants were fired. No one admitted to stealing the countess's jewels, and the countess never got any satisfaction before she died. But many, many years later, while some workmen were redoing the facade of the palazzo, hidden high up in the eaves, they came across a nest. Guess what they found inside it?

Charlie got to know Cliff when he began taking flying lessons that summer. The airport, as the crow flies, was only a few miles from the farm, and Charlie maintained that his whole entire life his ambition was to fly.

"Really?" I was skeptical.

"I hate to fly," I also said.

Charlie just laughed.

"Wait and see," he said. "Once I get my pilot's license, I'll take you to Rehoboth Beach."

Rehoboth Beach is a popular vacation destination. The wooden boardwalk is a mile long and lined with shops, restaurants, and attractions. Located near the boardwalk, the Rehoboth Beach Bandstand holds open-air concerts during the summer season.

Cliff owned a Cessna 172 Skyhawk. The Cessna 172 Skyhawk is a four-seat, single-engine, high-wing, fixed-wing aircraft.

"It's a safe plane," Charlie reported. "The Skyhawk has the best accident rate in private aviation."

After his flying lessons, Charlie started going up with Cliff. Additional instruction, I suppose. They didn't go far; they just flew around the county. One time they nearly ran out of gas as they were circling our farm—I was out riding and the plane was flying so low that my horse shied. They made it back to the airport just in time.

"You could have gotten me killed," I told Charlie when he got home.

"You're lucky we didn't get killed," Charlie answered.

One sock—buy him.
Two socks—try him.
Three socks—doubt him.
Four socks—do without him.
Four white feet and a white nose—knock him in the head and feed him
to the crows.

The old adage horsemen like to spout about horses' markings is dead wrong.

My nine-year-old chestnut mare, Esmeralda, Esmé for short, had four white stockings and a star on her forehead and was a sweetheart. I had had her for four years and she had calmed down a lot since we bought her. She had comfortable gaits and she could jump like "a toad in a thunderstorm"—who said that? Mark Twain? She was usually pretty calm and the only thing that really bothered her was a loud noise—a car door slamming or a gunshot. We were riding along the road one day when a truck went by and the driver blew his air horn at us, and, bucking, Esmé bolted and I nearly got thrown.

I read the part in *Wuthering Heights* where it is Nelly, the house-keeper, and not Catherine who tries to dispel Heathcliff's black mood by telling him: "You're fit for a prince in disguise. Who knows, but your father was Emperor of China, and your mother an Indian queen."*

The movie version with Laurence Olivier and Merle Oberon, directed by William Wyler, is, in fact, quite different from the novel.

---

* Brontë, *Wuthering Heights*, p. 58.

One afternoon when the weather—heavy rain and predicted thunderstorms—kept them from flying, Charlie brought Cliff home. The two men sat in the living room drinking bourbon and smoking cigars. (Charlie had a cache of contraband Cuban cigars.) The cigar smoke drove me out. Upstairs, I could hear the twins running from room to room, playing a noisy game, and I longed for something else—something different.

Cliff came to the door of the kitchen and stood watching me as I was starting to fix dinner.

"What are you cooking?" he asked.

"Beef bourguignon," I replied without looking up.

"A French dish," he said.

I didn't answer.

"Smells good," he said, before he turned around and left.

The next time Cliff came to the house, Charlie was still out feeding the horses and I let Cliff in.

"How's Sally?" I asked him.

"Don't know."

"Oh, why not?"

"I guess we're not seeing each other anymore." Then, after he had come inside and taken off his jacket, he said, "Happy?"

I shrugged and went back into the kitchen.

Cliff, I had heard, had a wife, but they were separated. He also had a son.

"So—how old is your son?" I asked, to change the subject.

"Alex is five."

We were both silent.

"What's for dinner?" he asked, following me into the kitchen.

"Spaghetti," I answered.

"Oh, I was hoping you would cook that French dish—what did you call it? Beef something."

Taking my arm, Cliff turned me to him and kissed me.

"Beef bourguignon," I said, when he let me go.

His fingers left marks on my forearm.

Recipe for Beef Bourguignon

6 ounces bacon
1 tablespoon olive oil
3 pounds lean stewing beef, cut into 2-inch cubes
1 carrot, peeled and sliced
1 onion, peeled and sliced
1 teaspoon salt
1/4 teaspoon freshly ground black pepper
2 tablespoons flour
3 cups red wine (preferably a Bordeaux or a Burgundy)
2 to 3 cups beef stock
1 tablespoon tomato paste
2 cloves garlic, mashed
1 sprig thyme
1 fresh bay leaf . . . etc.

Recipe for Spaghetti

Put a lot of water in a pot, bring to a boil, dump the spaghetti in the water, cook for about ten minutes, drain the spaghetti, done.

Soon Charlie and Cliff were fast friends. Charlie talked about Cliff all the time: *Cliff said this. Cliff did this. Cliff thinks this.* They even had some projects going together.

"What kind of projects?" I asked him.

"Real estate," Charlie answered. "He's got some property in downtown Charlottesville he wants to develop."

"And you are going to invest in it?"

"That's the idea," Charlie said.

"But what do you know about Cliff?

"Nothing," I added.

"He's smart and he has connections with people in town. Local people.

"Honey, please. Trust me," Charlie also said.

"And when I get my pilot's license, I am going to buy into his plane. We'll share it," Charlie said.

"A plane costs a small—"

But before I could finish my sentence, Charlie said, "We'll both fly you to Rehoboth Beach."

Nelly, my Norwich terrier, for an inexplicable reason liked Cliff. Each time he came to the house, she ran over to him, her stump of a tail wagging so hard I half expected it to fall off as he bent down to pat her. He made a big fuss over her. Then, still more inexplicably, she followed him into the living room.

"Nelly!" I called out to her. "Come. Come here," I commanded.

She paid no attention.

I think I heard Cliff laugh.

"Little whore," I muttered under my breath.

From the living room window, I watched them. Charlie and Cliff were leaning against the doors of their respective vehicles—Charlie's Ford pickup truck and Cliff's sleek blue Rover 2000 TC. They were talking but I could not hear what they were saying. I looked at them both, trying to imagine them as strangers and as if I were seeing them for the first time. Charlie was fair skinned—his hair almost reddish—and broad shouldered. He was wearing jeans, old brown cowboy boots, and a faded green baseball cap with the logo of a feed store on it. Cliff was dark skinned and lean. He was bare headed and his black hair was thick and wavy. He, too, was wearing jeans and a denim shirt. The sleeves of his shirt were rolled up tight and high enough to expose his upper arms. His biceps flexed as he struck a match to light a cigarette.

Already I had fallen for him, but I fell for him again then—hard.

Originally a pub, our brick house was built in the 1740s, and rumor had it that Thomas Jefferson and James Madison dined there. It has since been remodeled and enlarged several times. The warren of small rooms upstairs has been turned into three decent-sized bedrooms, and the downstairs, despite the low ceilings (guests over six feet tall are warned to duck their heads when they enter the living room), has been opened up so that the kitchen and dining area are one large room. The huge stone fireplace in the kitchen, in which, if we were so disposed, we could have roasted an ox, was original, as was the back staircase—the steps steep, narrow, and treacherous. (Once, slipping down those stairs when I was seven months pregnant, I was afraid I would miscarry.)

"The house consists of four rooms on each floor, and is two storeys high. When the Brontës took possession, they made the larger parlour, to the left of the entrance, the family sitting-room, while that on the right was appropriated to Mr Brontë as a study. Behind this was the kitchen, and behind the former, a sort of flagged store-room. Upstairs, there were four bedchambers of similar size . . ."

"The small first floor room over the hall . . . known as 'the children's study,' was also used as a bedroom by Emily."*

---

* "Inside Haworth: The Humble Parsonage Where the Brontë Sisters Changed Literature," *Country Life*, July 30, 2018, https://www.countrylife.co.uk/out-and-about/theatre-film-music/bronte-sisters -parsonage-haworth-146543.

"Do you know Cliff's wife?" I asked Meryl, my neighbor.

"I've met her," Meryl answered, nodding.

We were standing by the side of the road while Charlie was talking to Frank about buying horse feed. He was telling Frank that Cliff had recommended a store in Ruckersville.

"A lot cheaper there," Charlie was saying.

"I hear she wants sole custody of their kid," Meryl continued.

"Why?"

"I don't know exactly, but I hear he has quite a temper." Meryl gave a little laugh before she said, "Frank said that, last year, out on the hunting field, he saw Cliff nearly whip a horse to death because he wouldn't take a jump."

"Oh" was all I said.

"But Frank is prejudiced," Meryl went on. "He hasn't gotten over the fact that Cliff still owes him money for the diaper service for his kid. It's been nearly four years and he still hasn't paid Frank." Meryl shook her head and made a face.

I said nothing.

"Anyway, who knows what's true."

"What's Cliff's wife's name?"

"Daphne. She works in the Barracks Road Shopping Center, at the store that sells wool and sewing stuff," Meryl added.

"What does she look like?" I persisted.

"A redhead with lots of freckles. She's cute," Meryl also added.

In bed—only we were not in a bed, we were lying on a plaid blanket, amid our tossed clothing, in a deserted polo field—I asked:

"Where did you grow up?"

"All over," Cliff answered as he lit a cigarette, then, after taking a puff, handed it to me.

"No, seriously," I said, exhaling smoke and handing him back the cigarette.

"Seriously. My dad was in the navy."

Charlie and I started dating my freshman year in college; we got married after he graduated. I got pregnant right away with the twins and did not graduate. I had never been with anyone before Charlie. I had never slept with another man until Cliff.

I began to smoke more. From one or two cigarettes a day, I was up to almost a pack.

In the truck, the twins waved their hands around in the air and complained.

"Can't breathe," Sam said.

"Open the window then," I told him.

"I thought you were going to quit," Charlie said.

I shrugged.

"You smell like an ashtray," Charlie continued.

"Then don't come near me," I answered.

"What's that supposed to mean?" Charlie asked.

For some unnamed yet felt reason, Charlie and I had not had sex in weeks.

Knit & Stitch was the name of the store that sold wool and sewing supplies in the Barracks Road Shopping Center. A large straw basket filled with different-colored spools of wool was in the window.

I can hardly thread a needle or sew on a button. What would I tell Cliff's wife I was looking for?

A bell jingled when I opened the door.

Sitting behind the counter, the saleslady put down her knitting and stood up. She had long gray hair, had no visible freckles, and was overweight.

"Can I help you?" she asked.

On my way out of the shopping center parking lot, distracted, I backed the truck into a car. The car, a red BMW (brand-new, from the look of it), had been waiting to get into my spot and I had not seen it. I smashed the BMW's right headlight and part of the front fender and smashed my own left taillight.

The owner of the car was not happy as we traded car insurance information. Charlie, when I got home, was not happy either.

"The truck is old," he said. "It's going to be difficult to find a replacement for that taillight. They probably don't make them anymore. And if the police catch me without a working taillight, I can get fined. Worse still," Charlie continued, getting angrier, "if it rains and water gets inside the broken taillight it can fuck up the entire electrical system and we won't have anything more to drive."

"I'm sorry," I kept repeating.

"Didn't you at least look before you backed up?" Charlie also kept repeating.

In the end, Cliff found us the taillight. He knew a garage in Crozet owned by a black man named Jacob. Jacob, he said, sold a lot of secondhand car parts.

"Stolen car parts?" Charlie had asked, no longer quite as angry.

In the Rover, driving, Cliff told me how he got his tires.

"Simple. I rent a car for the day, a new Avis or a Hertz, then I switch the rental car's tires with the old ones on my car. No one ever notices." Cliff laughed.

I laughed, too.

"Mr. Earnshaw once bought a couple of colts at the parish fair, and gave the lads each one. Heathcliff took the handsomest, but it soon fell lame, and when he discovered it, he said to Hindley, 'You must exchange horses with me: I don't like mine . . .'" Nelly tells Mr. Lockwood, the tenant of Thrushcross Grange.*

* Brontë, *Wuthering Heights*, p. 39.

In my dreams, I was always driving too fast or flying too high. In one that I can still remember, I was somewhere I had never been before. A beautiful Caribbean resort, the kind you see in ads, overlooking a pristine white, sandy beach and the blue ocean with gentle lapping waves—all very idyllic—with couples cavorting in the water, drinking rum cocktails, smiling, happy, etc. I was sitting in a chaise longue and wearing a two-piece red-and-blue-striped bathing suit—unlike any I own—and I was there alone, but waiting, I think, for someone, when all of a sudden there was a tremendous roar as this gigantic dark wave rose up on the horizon. Everyone in the dream—all those happy couples—started to scream and I got up from the chaise longue and started to run. Run for my life. The other thing I remember about that dream is that the bra strap on my bathing suit broke when I got up to run.

"I've dreamt in my life dreams that have stayed with me ever after, and changed my ideas; they've gone through and through me, like wine through water, and altered the colour of my mind," Catherine Earnshaw tells Nelly.*

---

* Brontë, *Wuthering Heights*, p. 80.

I also remember that in a college art course I took, we were shown a slide of *The Great Wave off Kanagawa,* a nineteenth-century woodblock print by the Japanese artist Hokusai and part of his series *Thirty-Six Views of Mount Fuji.*

"My family moved to Japan, to Sasebo, when I was sixteen," Cliff told me. "Before that we lived on Lake Michigan at the Great Lakes Naval Station, where we froze our asses off. Everyone called it the 'Great Mistakes,'" Cliff said, giving a laugh that sounded more like a snort. "Japan was a big change."

Again, we were lying on the plaid blanket—the blanket he kept in the trunk of the Rover.

"Sasebo? Where's that?"

"On Kyushu Island. Not far from Nagasaki."

"Oh. Nagasaki. Did you go?"

"No. The city was off-limits to navy personnel. The fallout from the radiation was said to be too dangerous. Sasebo has a huge U.S. naval base," Cliff went on. "We were sent there a couple of years before the start of the Korean War. Why all these questions?" Cliff said as he tightened his arms around me and began to make love to me again.

Afterward, I said, "Did you learn to speak Japanese?"

There are two types of residual radioactivity after a nuclear explosion. One is the fallout from the nuclear material and fission products, but these are usually scattered in the atmosphere or blown away by the wind. (Thus the radioactivity in the black rain that may have fallen on the cities would have been very low.) The second form of radiation is neutron activation, but if the bombs are detonated from high altitudes, the risk of contamination is also minimal.

"And when did you join the navy?"

"After I got kicked out of college."

"Which college?"

"Harvard," Cliff answered, laughing.

"What did you get kicked out for?"

"A bunch of stuff—cheating, stealing, fornicating—take your pick."

"I'm serious."

On his right cheek—the cheek of his ass—Cliff had a tattoo. A brilliant green, red, and blue tattoo of a dragon.

"I got drunk. Some guys took me to a tattoo parlor."

"Where?"

"Hong Kong—we went there on leave."

Charlie laughed when I told him Cliff said he went to Harvard.

"Are you kidding me? What else did he tell you? That he was Alpha Beta Kappa? That he was a musical prodigy? That he graduated at age fourteen? Solved the fundamental law of the universe? Please, he's putting you on."

"Did he finish his education, on the Continent, and come back a gentleman? or did he get a sizar's place* at college? or escape to America, and earn honours by drawing blood from his foster country? or make a fortune more promptly, on the English highways?" Mr. Lockwood asks Nelly, eager for more details about his inhospitable landlord, Heathcliff.**

---

* A scholarship position at Cambridge University, such as the one held by Brontë's father at St. John's College.

** Brontë, *Wuthering Heights*, p. 92.

Wuthering Heights was lying on top of the coffee table in the living room and I saw Cliff pick it up. He examined the book, turning it over a couple of times.

"Who was Emily Brontë?" he asked, pronouncing "Brontë" in a peculiar way—"Bron-TIE."

Instead of correcting him, I began to explain how she and her sisters, Charlotte and Anne, lived with their father, a clergyman, in Haworth, a village situated on a remote and desolate moor in West Riding of Yorkshire, and how, despite their isolated lives, all three had managed to write books, when Charlie came into the room and I stopped speaking and Cliff put the book back down on the coffee table.

Only it wasn't over the book that it began—or only indirectly.

Cliff brought a couple of blue-winged teal ducks he had shot over to the house. He wanted to give them to Charlie, only Charlie wasn't home. The twins were already in bed, asleep.

"Will you give me a hand plucking them?" he asked me.

Stroking the bright blue wing feathers, I shook my head and said, "I am sorry you shot them."

He laughed and said, "Let's have a drink then."

We sat on the couch in the living room, drank wine, kissed, and made out—the little whore Nelly lying at Cliff's feet—until we heard Charlie drive up in the truck.

"'That's a turkey's [feather],' [Catherine] murmured to herself; 'and this is a wildduck's; and this is a pigeon's . . . And here is a moorcock's; and this—I should know it among a thousand—it's a lapwing's . . . Heathcliff set a trap over it and . . . I made him promise he'd never shoot a lapwing, after that, and he didn't.'"*

---

* Brontë, *Wuthering Heights*, pp. 122–23.

It is hard to describe how handsome Cliff was, how sexy, and how attracted I was to his lean, dark good looks, to his muscular body, to his hard, flat stomach, to even his tight tattooed ass. Also, his self-assurance, his confidence—the same thing, I suppose—and how he felt himself above the law. He was uninhibited and there was something dangerous about him that drew me. Something almost feral. And the fact, too, that he loved me. Truly loved me. It was exciting and astonishing. I had never felt anything like it.

"And after the navy what did you do?" I asked him.

"I robbed a bank."

"No, seriously."

"Seriously?" Cliff tightened his arms around me. "Seriously, I was looking for you."

"He neither spoke, nor loosed his hold, for some five minutes, during which period he bestowed more kisses than ever he gave in his life before . . ."*

---

* Brontë, *Wuthering Heights*, p. 159.

The Southwest Virginia Angus Association sale takes place three times a year at the Washington County Fairgrounds in Abingdon. Early one Saturday morning, Charlie decided to take the twins with him.

"Good experience for them," he told me. "They might learn something about cattle."

The twins were not convinced. They hated long car rides.

"I am going to be carsick," Sam said.

"Bring a paper bag," Charlie told him.

Pete made retching noises and laughed.

"You, too, bring a paper bag," Charlie said, "and I don't want to hear another word from either one of you. Hurry up, now. The sale starts at noon and we're going to be late."

From Charlottesville, Abingdon is 241 miles by car—
following I-64 and I-81—an approximately three-hour-
and-forty-two-minute drive. Crozet is fifteen miles from
downtown Charlottesville and another five miles from our
farm. Once Charlie and the twins had left, Cliff and I drove
to Crozet—on I-64, the same route Charlie had first taken
to go to Abingdon—in twenty minutes.

Jacob's garage was on Rockfish Gap Turnpike and Jacob
was happy to see Cliff. The two men embraced.

"You are a sight for sore eyes," Jacob told Cliff.

"This here is my friend," Cliff said, introducing me to
Jacob.

Jacob and I shook hands.

"A friend of Cliff's is a friend of mine," Jacob told me.

Jacob's face was dark and creased and his front tooth was
gold. He smiled as he held my hand in his.

"So what do you need?" he asked Cliff.

"Let's go get something to eat first," Cliff said.

The diner was a couple of blocks from the garage. We ate
fried-chicken burgers and drank Dr Peppers. Cliff and I, the
only white people having lunch there.

After lunch we drove to Lynchburg on the Blue Ridge Parkway.

"Do you know why the Blue Ridge Mountains look blue?" I asked Cliff.

"Tell me," he said.

Holding me close to him, he drove with one hand.

"The trees release isoprene into the atmosphere, which makes the mountains look hazy and blue."

"Is that so," Cliff said. "Good to know."

A few miles outside Lynchburg, near Appomattox, Cliff got us a room in a motel. The room cost forty-two dollars a night. Only it was the afternoon.

"I love the word," I told Cliff, repeating it. "Appomattox."

"I love you," Cliff said.

Although the end of September, it was still hot and humid when we got ready to leave. The motel looked deserted; Cliff's Rover was the only car parked out front. The pool, too, was empty. On an impulse, we jumped into the water fully dressed.

"Hey!"

The motel manager suddenly appeared at the office door.

"Hey!" he repeated, shouting, "You can't go in the pool with your clothes on!"

"We'll take them off," Cliff shouted back.

"A bunch of scofflaws," the motel manager yelled at us as we drove off.

On the way home, sitting in our wet clothes, I said, "I don't expect Charlie and the twins back until late tonight, but you never know."

"Don't worry. You'll be home in plenty of time."

I liked the way Cliff drove. He drove fast, double-clutching to change gears.

"Will you teach me how?" I asked him once.

"Sure. It's easy."

"What about Alex, your son?" I also asked.

"What about him?"

"Where does he go to school?"

"He goes to that expensive Montessori school in town. Daphne insisted," Cliff answered.

"Daphne—"

"Yeah. Daphne, my wife. My soon-to-be ex-wife," Cliff said. "The kids sit on their little individual rugs all day and learn nothing. A big waste of money," Cliff continued.

"Pete and Sam go to public school," I said after a while to fill in the silence. "Maybe next year, when they go to middle school, we'll send them to private school. That is, if we can afford it," I added.

"I thought you guys were rich," Cliff said.

"Will you marry me?" Cliff also said.

"*Wuthering Heights* is a virgin's story . . . The love the two feel for each other is a longing for an impossible completion."*

---

* Elizabeth Hardwick, *Seduction and Betrayal: Women and Literature* (New York: New York Review of Books, 2001), p. 9.

It was midnight before Charlie got home, and both boys were already fast asleep in the truck. Lifting each of them out of the cab, Charlie and I took Sam and Pete upstairs to their bedroom, where we half undressed them and put them to bed.

"What did you do all day while we were gone?" Charlie asked as he was taking off Sam's shoes.

"Not much," I answered.

"I went for a ride," I lied.

Lies, lies, lies:

- *I need to borrow the truck to go to the grocery store. We are nearly out of milk.*
- *I have to use the truck to pick up some cough medicine at the pharmacy. I think Sam is coming down with something.*
- *I promised to meet [name of a friend] for lunch and I said I would drive her to Farmington.*
- *I have an appointment at the hairdresser—I haven't had my hair cut in months.*
- *I rescheduled the meeting with Sam and Pete's homeroom teacher at school for this afternoon . . .*

I got good at telling them.

Separated from his wife, Cliff was still living at home—he was sleeping on the sofa in the den, he said.

"It's like sleeping on Chattahoochee deck paving," he complained. "The springs are shot."

"Chattahoo—what?" I started to ask.

He also said that he was getting divorced, only Daphne was creating problems. She was accusing him of an affair with Sally. She didn't have proof yet, but she was using her female instinct—Cliff rolled his eyes and gave a laugh. The reason for the divorce, she threatened, was adultery. He might then be deemed an unfit parent and lose custody of Alex.

"She can be totally irrational," Cliff said about Daphne.

In the South, pebble paving is known as Chattahoochee. Chattahoochee is also the Creek Indian word for "river of painted rocks."

A few of the places we found to make love:

- *In the deserted polo field—weather permitting—on the plaid blanket*
- *In a motel room outside Gordonsville, a town where we knew no one*
- *In a trailer—only once—that belonged to a friend of Cliff's, the inside a mess of dirty dishes in the sink and clothes on the floor*
- *In our guest room the three nights Charlie was down in Florida visiting his parents and the boys were in bed asleep*
- *In the back seat of the Rover, like teenagers . . .*

"Heathcliff is—an unreclaimed creature, without refinement —without cultivation; an arid wilderness of furze and whin-stone. I'd as soon put that little canary into the park on a winter's day as recommend you to bestow your heart on him!" is how Catherine describes Heathcliff to Isabella, her sister-in-law, in order to dissuade her from marrying him.*

---

* Brontë, *Wuthering Heights*, p. 102.

According to Charlie, Cliff owned a bunch of derelict rental buildings in downtown Charlottesville. Their plan was to raze them and, in their stead, build a couple of apartment buildings.

"Cheap but good housing for low-income people," Charlie said.

"You mean for blacks," I said.

"For everyone," Charlie said.

"Right," I said.

"And how are you going to get the money to do that?" I also asked.

"I spoke to my dad," Charlie answered.

Once a week, Alice Washington's husband dropped her off at our house at eight o'clock in the morning before he, too, went to work. In the afternoon when she finished cleaning— before Pete and Sam came home from school—I drove her into town so she could catch the bus home.

"Do you have kids?" I had asked her.

"Yes, ma'am," she answered.

"How many?"

In the truck, Alice Washington sat very straight, holding her leather purse on her lap. Older than I, Alice must have been in her forties. A big woman, she was strong—I had watched her easily move heavy furniture—and her dark hair was curly and short.

"Mostly, they're grown," she said. "Only one is still at home."

"Who's that?"

"Malcolm. He's in high school. A junior."

Usually we rode in silence.

"Your husband works at the hospital?" I once asked her.

"Yes, ma'am, he does."

"Does he like his job?"

"Yes, ma'am. He's worked there for over twenty years."

"How come he can't come and pick you up?" I also ventured to ask her.

Alice hesitated before she answered: "He works late sometimes and I have to get back and start supper."

Another time, when we got to the bus depot, I asked, "Alice, do you have time for a cup of coffee with me?"

"No, ma'am. Thank you. I've got to get along home."

Then, after dropping her off, I once again drove to the Barracks Shopping Center and to the Knit & Stitch shop. This time, the store was shut, and instead of the colored spools of wool on display in the window, there was a FOR LEASE sign.

Alice! Have you ever had an affair?
Alice! Have you ever cheated on your husband?
Alice! Alice!

One morning in October we trailered our horses and drove over to Keswick for the first foxhunt of the season. Esmé got into the trailer quietly, as did—more or less—Charlie's horse. A big seventeen-hand dark bay named Dallas, he could, at times, be a bit unruly, but that day we drove without trouble and the horses were quiet. Charlie and I both preferred the Keswick Hunt to the Farmington Hunt, as there was more open land to ride on. The land available to the Keswick Hunt ranged over five counties and included thirty-five square miles.

"Last time I rode over here," Charlie said, "I never once saw a house."

"That's bound to change soon," I said.

Charlie glanced over at me and started to say something but changed his mind. We drove the rest of the way in silence.

After parking the horse trailer and truck and saddling our horses, we joined the group of a dozen or so horses and their riders who had gathered in front of the clubhouse; to one side, the pack of hounds was barking excitedly around the huntsman.

The first rider I recognized was Sally. A whipper-in, she was smartly dressed in a Pink coat—the coats are actually red but called pink (the term "pink" comes from Mr. Pink, the tailor who made the hunting coats). Her horse, a gray—the gray, I recognized, Cliff had ridden in the steeplechase—was acting up and she was having trouble controlling him. She kept circling him with a tight rein so that he would not take off or buck. I watched as Charlie rode up to her.

"I don't know what's gotten into him," I heard her say.

"Do you want to trade horses?" Charlie asked Sally. "I can ride him and you can take Dallas."

At the time, I remember thinking Charlie was unusually solicitous. He was having an affair with Sally.

Foxhunting etiquette:

- *Never take rides on hunt or non-hunt days through hunting territory unless you have permission from the landowner(s) and have called to make sure the area you wish to ride in is open.*

- *Because we are representing the Keswick Hunt Club each time we go out, make sure your horse is fit and ready to hunt and is clean and properly turned out.*

- *Put a red ribbon in the tail of a horse who kicks (and keep to the rear) and a green ribbon in the tail of a green horse.*

- *You should be clean and neat as well. There are opportunities to get dirty along the way.*

- *If you have long hair, you must wear a hair net—male or female.*

- *Rated safety helmets are strongly recommended and all helmet chin straps should be securely fastened.*

- *Tack should be of black or brown leather, with a white saddle pad, preferably contoured, not square. No colored pads, boots, wraps, fleece, etc., especially on formal days.**

---

* "Etiquette," Keswick Hunt Club, https://www.keswickhuntclub.com/fox-hunting/etiquette.

"So what was the problem with Sally's horse?" I asked Charlie at the end of the hunt.

I was riding close enough to Charlie to see that the gray horse was running smoothly and taking all the fences.

"Sally said something about Cliff overriding him," Charlie answered.

I said nothing.

In the truck, on the way home, Charlie said, "You know what else Sally told me?"

"No, no idea."

"She told me she used to hunt with William Faulkner when Faulkner lived in Charlottesville. She said he wasn't a good rider, but he was fearless."

"Thanks to alcohol," I said.

"His horse was called Powerhouse," Charlie added.

"Life among the fox hunters was a form of acceptance for Faulkner into the higher reaches of American society . . . There was money, position, background, and family lines; and the group favored plenty of whiskey along with the riding. Most of all there was tradition. Faulkner loved to put on the full regalia . . . He equally embraced the formalities: the prehunt breakfast, the coming together of men and women who loved their horses, the posthunt parties, and the hard drinking which accompanied everything. He also admired the daring, the taking of obstacles on a big horse which required a timing and a strength which were beyond him . . . he apparently needed that physical goad to stir himself, even at the expense of broken limbs . . ."*

---

* Frederick R. Karl, *William Faulkner: American Writer; A Biography* (New York: Weidenfeld & Nicolson, 1989), p. 989.

In Albemarle County, Sally's car was instantly recognizable. She drove a dark green Jaguar with an ornament on its hood— a silver-plated statue of a horse. Soon after the day I had seen her at the hunt, word spread throughout Charlottesville that the hood ornament of the horse on her car had been stolen.

"She's very upset about it," Charlie told me.

"In fact, she is obsessed and determined to find the culprit. She said that her husband had had the horse statue made specifically for her as a birthday present. The horse is solid silver, not just silver-plated, and valuable," Charlie continued.

"I wonder who stole it," I said.

"Whoever did made a big mess of it, too. The entire hood needs to be replaced," Charlie said.

"You saw the car?" I asked.

"She's been to the police about it," Charlie answered.

Sally asked Charlie to stable and school the gray horse for her. His name was Barneys Joy.

"Who's Barney?" I asked Charlie.

Charlie said he did not know. He said he thought Barneys Joy was the name of a place not a person.

Because I assumed the Jaguar was being repaired, Sally drove over to our farm in her old wood-paneled station wagon, a 1951 Ford Country Squire. She wanted to check on her horse, she said.

"Have you seen Cliff lately?" I couldn't resist asking her.

"He and Charlie are planning a redevelopment in downtown Charlottesville," I went on, heedless.

"Charlie should be careful," Sally said. "Cliff owes me money. He promised to pay me back by the end of last month, but I have yet to see a penny of it."

"What does 'Barneys Joy' stand for?" I asked, to change the subject.

"I like grays," I also told her.

In 1943, the U.S. government built the Barneys Joy Point Military Reservation on land it had acquired. The purpose was to protect the Cape Cod Canal from possible air and naval attack during World War II.

In spite of what Sally and Meryl had said, Charlie kept defending Cliff.

"Cliff claims the diapers were dirty. The reason he didn't pay. He said that 'the diapers were full of shit'—literally. Each time, his wife had to rewash them. Who can blame him? The guy's not an ass."

Again, I said nothing.

Have you seen the tattoo of a dragon he got in the navy?

Charlie was lucky. As a working farmer, he was exempted from the draft.

Cliff spent two years in the navy—he was only nineteen when he enlisted—and, for a year, he was stationed in the Philippines.

"I had a blast," he told me.

"I think I was drunk most of the time," he also said. "The women, too, were amazing."

"What women?" I asked.

"The Filipino women."

We were in bed in the Gordonsville's motel room. "Don't worry," Cliff said, laughing. "They didn't hold a candle to you, baby."

"*Can't hold a candle to* is an idiom, which is a word, group of words or phrase that has a figurative meaning that is not easily deduced from its literal meaning. The phrase *can't hold a candle to* has its roots in the 1600s, when the lowly apprentice to a master of a craft might only be fit to hold a candle in order to provide light for the master while he tends to a problem. An apprentice who was not even skillful enough to hold a candle for his master was worthless, indeed."*

---

* "Can't Hold a Candle To," Grammarist, http://grammarist.com/idiom/cant-hold -a-candle-to.

"Have they found out who stole the hood ornament off Sally's car?" I asked Charlie.

"No. They haven't found out yet," Charlie answered, shrugging his shoulders.

When I asked Cliff the same thing, he shook his head and laughed. "No," he said, "and they probably never will."

Falling out of a tree, Sam broke his leg.

"What were you thinking, letting him climb up that tree?" I asked Carol, who had been babysitting.

Not able to distinguish between the two boys, she was still unsure which twin was hurt.

At Martha Jefferson Hospital, Dr. Nicoll x-rayed and set Sam's leg.

"I'm working on an inflatable splint," he told Sam as he was applying the plaster. "It will be much lighter and easier to use. I've been trying it out on one of my horses who broke his leg, and so far, it is working fine."

"How did your horse break his leg?" Sam asked.

"It's a clean break," Dr. Nicoll told me. "He should be as good as gold again in six weeks." British and good-looking, Dr. Nicoll spoke with a distinguished accent. "He's a brave little lad," he added, patting Sam on the head.

Sam had not cried once.

"And it was lovely to meet you," Dr. Nicoll told me as we were getting ready to leave.

"We'll meet again soon, I hope," he also said, as he held on to my hand.

Little Dorrit was the book, I noticed, Carol had been reading.

"But on March 14, riding his huge mount, Powerhouse, he fell from the horse while making a turning maneuver and broke his clavicle. Yet even this did not prevent him from enjoying his day; for by later afternoon, his shoulder bandaged, his right arm in a sling, he was back riding. He made light of it, telling Dr. Nicoll, who treated him in Charlottesville, that his strength was returning."*

* Karl, *William Faulkner, American Writer*, p. 994.

Two days later I was back in Dr. Nicoll's office.

Not for what he had perhaps hoped, but because, in my rush, I had slammed the truck door on my hand.

My hand was swollen and painful, but no bones were broken, Dr. Nicoll assured me, his interest in me gone.

Cliff, when he saw my hand, kissed each sore and swollen finger and said Dr. Nicoll was a jerk.

On the way home from school one afternoon, Pete asked me, "How did the cowboy ride into town on Friday, stay for three days, and ride out on Friday?"

Pete liked telling jokes.

"I don't know," I said. "How did he?"

"His horse's name was Friday," Pete answered.

"Get it?"

Meryl, my neighbor, was my friend and I did not want to complain to her about her daughter Carol.

Nevertheless, I thought Carol had been negligent—her nose in a book instead of paying attention to the twins.

"Find another babysitter then," Charlie said when I mentioned it to him.

"Who?"

"I don't know. The housekeeper. Alice. Alice what's-her-name."

"Her name is Alice Washington," I said.

"Like George Washington. Remember him?" I added.

"What is wrong with you?" Charlie said.

"You have your period or what?"

No, I did not have my period. But what—of course, I took precautions—if I did get pregnant? And whose baby would it be anyway?

In the mid-1960s, surveys in New York City revealed various methods used to cause abortions. Women swallowed a range of toxic solutions such as turpentine, bleach, and detergents; they inserted foreign bodies into their vaginas such as coat hangers, knitting needles, pens, and rubber catheters; they took scalding baths, threw themselves down the stairs, all in their efforts to end unwanted pregnancies.

When I voiced my concern to Cliff, he again said, "Marry me."

After overhearing Catherine tell Nelly, "It would degrade me to marry Heathcliff, now," but before hearing the rest of her speech, "so he shall never know how I love him; and that, not because he's handsome, Nelly, but because he's more myself than I am," Heathcliff abruptly leaves Wuthering Heights.*

---

* Brontë, *Wuthering Heights*, p. 81.

Charlie confessed that he had taken out a loan at the bank. He used the farm as collateral.

"But the farm belongs to your dad," I said.

"Yes, but we have the same name and the bank officer did not know that. He was new.

"A young guy," Charlie added.

"You forged his signature?"

Charlie did not answer.

"And what did your dad say when you went down to Florida?"

"He said he would think about it."

"Can't you get into trouble for doing that?" I also asked. "I mean, what if your father finds out? Isn't that embezzlement or something—the misappropriation of funds?

"You could go to jail," I said.

Cliff came over to the house a lot, arriving unannounced at odd hours, to talk to Charlie. Sometimes he helped Charlie with the farmwork—mucking out the stalls, feeding the cattle, and watering the horses. Several times, he stayed for supper and he and Charlie talked about contractors, builders, town ordinances, certificates, while I tried to ignore him.

It felt like a game.

Another game we played was based on Cliff usually knowing where Charlie was when Charlie was not home.

With Sally.

But the problem was the babysitter. I was free only during the day when the twins were at school.

On the way back from the motel in Gordonsville one afternoon, the Rover got a flat tire. We skidded off Route 20, nearly ending up in a ditch.

"Damn," Cliff said. "That Hertz tire is crap."

I stood by the side of the road as Cliff jacked up the car to change the tire. To make matters worse, it began to rain.

"I'm going to be late picking up the twins," I told Cliff.

The twins, when I finally drove up in the truck, were not waiting for me at the end of the driveway and by the side of the road the way they always did. Instead, I saw them trudging along halfway up the drive—our driveway was nearly half a mile long—Sam hobbling on his crutches and both boys lugging their heavy backpacks.

"We're wet," Sam said.

"Where were you?" Pete asked.

I got to ride Barneys Joy once. I rode him in the ring and took a few jumps with him. A powerful, excitable horse, he was very different from Esmé. I had to adjust my seat, my hands, my feet. Instead of how I rode Esmé—loose reins, long stirrups—I had to ride him differently.

Charlie was standing in the middle of the ring shouting instructions at me.

"Don't pull the reins back. Squeeze your hands and bend your wrists. Let him feel the bit.

"In French, it's called *la déscente de la main*," he added.

"*Merci bien!*" I shouted back.

"I want you to engage his back. Make Barneys Joy lift his back, that way he stays more connected," Charlie shouted again as I had the horse canter and do figure eights in the ring.

"Be sure to shorten his approach stride," Charlie yelled when I was getting ready to jump him.

I could feel Barneys Joy's impulsion in both my feet and legs and all the way up to my groin as he shifted his gait to engage his hindquarters, push off the ground, and take the fence.

When I dismounted, my legs were shaking.

"You did good," Charlie said, taking the horse's bridle.

"Where did you learn to ride?" I once asked Cliff while he was shaking out the plaid blanket and we were getting ready to leave the polo field.

"In the navy," he replied, laughing.

"No, seriously."

"Seriously? I just picked it up when I moved here. I started out exercising polo ponies for a friend of Daphne's, then I began playing. It's fun. We have matches here most Sundays if we get enough riders and horses. Come by and watch."

I did not talk to Cliff about his business deal with Charlie.
Number one: I did not believe that it would work.
Number two: I knew what Charlie had done was illegal.
Number three: I knew that Cliff owed people money.
Number four: I did not want to think about it.

Number five: I had heard it said—again from Meryl—how Cliff had nearly gone to jail once for selling cockfighting supplies. Apparently, federal agents had raided a "cockpit" in Greenwood, Virginia, and had indicted him on three counts.

Count 1 alleged that Cliff was conducting an illegal gambling business involving cockfighting, in violation of Virginia law and 18 U.S.C. § 1955. Count 2 charged Cliff with conspiracy to sell and deliver in interstate commerce sharp instruments designed or intended to be attached to the leg of a bird for use in an animal fighting venture, in violation of 7 U.S.C. § 2156(e). Count 3 charged Cliff with the substantive crime of abetting the sponsoring of "an animal fighting venture," in violation of the laws of the Commonwealth of Virginia, 18 U.S.C. § 2, and 18 U.S.C. § 1955.

In the end, however, Cliff was acquitted on several grounds: (a) that the government's evidence was insufficient, (b) that the grand jury failed to allege the legal elements of the federal crimes in Counts 1 and 3, (c) that the evidence failed to establish a violation of the Virginia statutes set forth in Count 1, and (d) that the government failed to establish the necessary connection with interstate commerce to support a conviction under Count 2.

In West Virginia and in the neighboring counties of Kentucky and Virginia, cockfighting occurs on an organized scale and is accepted locally. Gambling is rampant and customary, while the presence of law enforcement varies.

Instead, in the Rover, on the way to and from our assignations, Cliff and I talked about "our" future life together.

"We can go live in Manteo, on Roanoke Island," he told me. "Have you been?"

I shook my head.

"The Outer Banks are beautiful, and I know a house there that's for rent. It belongs to a friend of mine. The house is by the ocean. You'll like it, I promise you," Cliff said.

"Manteo is named after an Indian who went to England with Sir Walter Raleigh and was baptized," Cliff also said.

"How do you know this?" I asked.

"Everyone knows this," Cliff answered, putting his arm around me.

"What about the Lost Colony?" I also asked.

"We would live simply. I could get a boat and trawl for shrimp. I like to fish," Cliff continued, not answering.

"Were the colonists murdered by Indians?

"And what about poor little Virginia Dare?" I added.

"People say that the colonists ran out of food and went to live with the Indians. Later, lots of blue-eyed Indians showed up in the area."

And what would I do all day in the house by the ocean in Manteo while Cliff was out fishing?

    And what about the twins?

"He's not a rough diamond—a pearl-containing oyster of a rustic; he's a fierce, pitiless, wolfish man," Nelly warns Isabella, Catherine's sister-in-law.*

---

* Brontë, *Wuthering Heights*, p. 102.

Cliff took the twins up in his plane one afternoon when they didn't have school. He flew them to Richmond. From the airport, they took a taxi to the Museum of the Confederacy, and from there, they went to Howard Johnson's, where the twins each got an ice cream cone, before they flew back.

"It was neat," Pete said. "We got to see Andrew Jackson's sword, and on the way over, we got to see my school and the soccer field."

"We saw these two bullets that collided in midair that—" Sam started to say.

"Cliff said that doesn't happen very often," Pete interrupted.

"But he said that it was a good thing, too, because it meant that the soldiers who fired those bullets did not get killed," Sam continued.

"We didn't get sick," Pete added, "and Cliff let me steer the plane."

"And which of the twenty-eight ice cream flavors did you pick?" I asked.

Banana, black raspberry, burgundy cherry, butter pecan, buttercrunch, butterscotch, etc., etc.

"What about Cliff's wife, Daphne?" I asked Charlie as we were driving into town one afternoon.

"What about her?"

"Have you met her?"

"I met her once."

"What's she like?"

"I don't know. I told you I only met her once."

"Still, you can get a feeling of what someone is like even if you just meet them once."

Instead of answering me, Charlie shrugged his shoulders.

Then I said, "Have you ever been to a cockfight?"

"Why?" Charlie frowned, and turning to look at me, he let the truck cross the road's median strip.

"Watch out," I said.

"Why do you want to know?" Charlie asked again, steering the truck back into our lane.

"Just curious," I said.

"Cockfights are illegal," Charlie said.

"I know. But have you been to one?"

Charlie paused before he said, "Yeah, once. It was pretty ugly."

"Where was it?" I persisted.

"I don't know. Outside of Charlottesville somewhere. In Greenwood, I think. A guy there raises fighting cocks."

"And who did you go with?"

"All these damn questions," Charlie said, shaking his head before adding, "No one you know."

Speeding up and honking the truck's horn, Charlie passed the car in front of us along a blind curve in the road.

The real estate Cliff owned was in downtown Charlottesville, a part of the city I had never been in. It consisted of a block of dilapidated houses. The sidewalk there was strewn with garbage—bottles, cans, papers. The houses' concrete steps were broken; the porches were cluttered with discarded appliances and cheap plastic toys; and most of the windows were boarded up. One house displayed a sign on the door—BEWARE OF THE DOG. As I drove slowly by in the truck, a young boy with an Afro came out of one of the houses and shouted at me: "You lost, lady? Or you—"

The rest of what he said was lost as I accelerated and sped off.

"What were you doing, driving over there?" Charlie asked me after I told him I had gone to see the houses they were going to replace with apartment buildings.

"It's a pretty dicey neighborhood," he continued. "We're having a hell of a time getting rid of some of the tenants—tenants, ha! They haven't paid rent in years. They're all drug addicts and alcoholics. We turned off all the utilities—electricity, water, phone—a long time ago. Demolition is scheduled to start next week."

"Demolition": From the sixteenth-century French *démoliss*, borrowed from the Latin *dēmōlīrī*—to defeat, to rout.

Je suis en train de démolir mon mariage . . .

(I took four years of high school French with Mademoiselle Blériot.)

Louise de Bassompierre, a classmate of the Brontës' at the school in Belgium, recorded her memories of the sisters: *"Miss Emily était beaucoup moins brillante que sa soeur mais bien plus sympathique."**

* Winifred Gérin, *Emily Brontë: A Biography* (Oxford: Clarendon Press, 1971), p. 131.

Charlie left before dawn one morning, taking Bella and Lela, the springer spaniels, to go duck hunting. When later he got home he complained: "I set up decoys and saw two bunches of ducks—buffleheads—fly by overhead, but the damn ducks kept right on going. I never got in a single shot."

Good, I was tempted to say.

Instead I asked him why he was no longer taking flying lessons.

"Not enough time," he answered.

"You have time to go hunting," I told him.

I was going to say something else, but the look Charlie gave me shut me up.

The twins got the chicken pox.

They each had a temperature of 102 and coughed. Then the rash appeared and the itching started.

"Try not to scratch," I kept repeating, "or you will scar."

I tried various remedies to relieve them: aloe, calamine lotion, a poultice of baking soda and water. I tried to make the twins wear cotton gloves.

Thank God Alice was able to help me out. She came every day for a few hours, and we took turns giving the twins oatmeal baths.

"It works best for the itching," she told me. "I used it on my children when they got the chicken pox."

Cliff could not remember whether he had had the chicken pox as a child and he worried that his son, Alex, would catch it. Alex, he said, was not a strong kid and susceptible to all kinds of illnesses—colds, earaches, sore throats—and Cliff stopped coming over to our house.

The term "chicken pox" is said to originate from either chickpeas or chicken pecks, which the sores are supposed to resemble.

I left the twins with Alice one afternoon and went riding. I needed to get out of the house and breathe fresh air. I persuaded Charlie to come with me.

"It'll do you good," I told him. "Take your mind off the construction site."

But after we had saddled up our horses and mounted them and were going down our driveway at a fast trot, he noticed that his horse Dallas was lame.

"Go on without me," Charlie said, turning his horse around and going back to the barn at a walk.

October had turned cold. Cold for Virginia, and too cold to make love on the plaid blanket outside in the polo field.

To make matters worse, Cliff's Rover was in the garage—the worn-out brake pads, he said, needed to be replaced.

Sally's Jaguar was repaired and she sent someone over to our farm with a horse trailer to pick up Barneys Joy.

"She's not coming over herself?" I asked Charlie.

"She's left town. She's gone to Italy, to a castle somewhere in Tuscany," Charlie said.

I wanted to confront Charlie about his affair, but I didn't. People in glass houses should not throw stones, etc., etc., etc.

He might have denied it or he might have said:
  And, anyway, who told you I was having an affair with Sally?
  A little birdie?
  A cuckoo.

Work on the site in downtown Charlottesville had begun. A local architect had redrawn the plans for the apartment buildings multiple times; a contractor had been hired, then fired. The second one still had to finish another job.

When I asked Charlie how things were going, either he did not answer or he said there were still a few problems that he and Cliff had to iron out. He also said for me to please stop pestering him about it. "Fucking pestering" is how he put it.

Partnership is far more difficult to maintain than marriage. Whereas 50 percent of marriages end in divorce, the number is closer to 80 percent for business partnerships.

As for maintaining our marriage:

In bed, Charlie tugged at my nightgown and tried to have sex with me. Most nights I made up the usual sort of excuse:

I have a headache.

I'm too tired.

I have my period—not that that, in the past, would have stopped him.

I have to go check on Pete and Sam.

One time I said, "I think I forgot to turn off the stove. I have to go down to the kitchen and look."

When I got back to the bedroom, Charlie was fast asleep.

Another time I said, "I forgot to lock the front door."

After the death of Catherine Earnshaw, I lost some of my interest in *Wuthering Heights*. I did not like the younger Catherine—she struck me as spoiled and silly. As for her husband, Linton, he was mean and sickly. Their marriage seemed a travesty. As for Heathcliff himself, he was behaving more obsessively and with more violence and cruelty. Also, I found it hard to concentrate on the novel—or on anything but Cliff.

Oh, thy bright eyes must answer now,
When Reason, with a scornful brow,
Is mocking at my overthrow!
Oh, thy sweet tongue must plead for me
And tell, why I have chosen thee!*

---

* Brontë, *Complete Poems*, p. 22.

After dropping Alice off at the bus depot one afternoon, I drove downtown again. I was curious to see the work that was being done on the site. The houses were gone; in their place was a large hole in the ground—it had rained recently and the hole was filled with water. Two bulldozers lined the street, a big ball and chain hung from a crane, but otherwise the street was quiet.

"How's the construction coming along?" Despite his warning, I couldn't resist asking Charlie again.

"The weather's been a bit of a problem," he answered, not looking at me.

Irritable and, no doubt, worried, Charlie was drinking too much. He started in as soon as he got home, with a tall glass of bourbon, neat. He ate little, he did not always bother to shave, and, easily provoked, he yelled at the twins.

Up in our bedroom, he kicked off his boots and let his clothes fall to the floor.

Before I had even opened my mouth to say something, he said, "Stop bitching and I'll pick them up in the morning."

Then he got into bed. He always slept naked.

Healed, but still in quarantine and not yet allowed to go back to school, the twins were home. They were restless and boisterous.

"Don't you have homework to do?" I asked.

"We've done it," Sam said.

"What about a book? What about *James and the Giant Peach*—have you read it?" I continued.

"I like the part where the parents get eaten by a rhinoceros," Pete said.

"And I like the part where the peach rolls down the hill, destroying everything along the way," Sam said.

To make matters worse, it rained solidly for several days and they could not go outside and play.

For a week, I did not see or hear from Cliff, and every afternoon, in spite of the pouring rain, I walked down our half-mile-long driveway—a Patsy Cline song obsessively replaying in my head—to the main road in the hope that he might be there, in his car, parked, waiting.

I fall to pieces
Each time I see you again
I fall to pieces . . .

"He's always, always in my mind—not as a pleasure, any more than I am always a pleasure to myself—but, as my own being—so, don't talk of our separation again—it is impracticable . . ." Catherine tells Nelly about Heathcliff.*

---

* Brontë, *Wuthering Heights*, pp. 82–83.

When, at last, Cliff called, Pete answered the phone.

"Mom!" he called. "It's Cliff. I told him Dad wasn't home, but he said he wanted to speak to you."

"Hello." I could hardly breathe or speak.

Nelly was barking as Sam was chasing her around the room. "Stop, please," I managed to tell him so I could hear.

"Can you meet me?" Cliff said. "I need to see you."

Yes, I will go live in the house by the ocean in Manteo.
   Yes, I will marry you.
   Yes.

Arriving late, Charlie, the twins, and I stood among the trailers and the grooms holding the horses and the tackle, only a few feet away from where the game was being played—played on *our* polo field.

"Stay right here next to me and Dad," I told the twins, "and hold my hand," I also said, but they didn't.

Leaning half out of the saddle, Cliff was in the middle of a furious melee of horseflesh, pounding hooves, jangling bridles, and swinging mallets. He wore a black T-shirt and the back of the T-shirt was stained with perspiration. From time to time, he and the whole field galloped toward us before they wheeled around and galloped off in another direction in pursuit of the ball.

In between chukkers, Cliff rode over to where we were standing and dismounted. Pulling out a red bandanna from his pants pocket, he wiped his face with it as he walked over to Sam and Pete and, bending down, said something that made the twins laugh. Then taking the reins of his horse— a fresh horse, another gray but a mare this time, who had red ribbons tied in her braided mane and tail—he mounted with the same single leap, and before he was properly settled in the saddle or had his feet in the stirrups—the gray mare already turning and moving toward the field—he looked back, smiled, and waved his mallet at us.

On the way home in the truck, I asked the twins, "What did Cliff say to you?"

"He told us a joke. A funny joke," Pete said.

"What was it?" I asked again.

Instead of answering, Pete said, "When I'm older, I want to play polo."

The red bandanna had been mine. I had worn it to keep the hair out of my face one warm day in the Rover with the windows open and Cliff had taken it from me without asking.

Every year Charlie's parents came up to the farm to celebrate Thanksgiving with us. This year their visit was canceled.

"Is your dad sick?" I asked Charlie. "Or your mom?"

"Too much going on here," Charlie answered, shaking his head. "Construction has just started and I have to be there most days."

"So what did you tell them?" I asked him.

Charlie did not answer.

"Just us then for dinner?" I said after a pause.

"Yeah, I can ask Cliff."

I was fond of Charlie's parents, a generous and friendly couple, and would miss them both. They made a big fuss over the twins, praised my cooking, and were generally undemanding. They didn't regret not living on the farm or in Virginia; life in Sarasota, Florida, was simpler and more fun, they claimed. My father-in-law had taken up golf, and my mother-in-law played bridge and collected shells, which she turned into jewelry, boxes, and frames. Each year, she brought me one of her artifacts. (I have all of them still.)

At the last minute, my parents, both Quakers, drove down from Massachusetts. At the start of Thanksgiving dinner, they had us hold hands around the table. On one side, I held my father's hand; on the other, Cliff's—he squeezed my hand so hard, my wedding ring dug painfully into my fingers. We all bowed our heads and were silent for a moment, while the twins tried to suppress their giggles.

The principal at the local high school, my father was bookish and quiet and I was close to him. My mother, an elementary teacher at a different school in the same town, tended to be too talkative and too inquisitive. Often, I was irritated by her. At dinner, the mood, given the recent national tragedy, was somber. Except perhaps sensing that things were also amiss here, my mother, nervous, never stopped talking.

"What recipe do you use for the stuffing?" she asked me, and, "How long did you cook the turkey? I cook mine for twenty minutes per pound."

"How big is the herd?" she asked Charlie. "And do you have to milk the cows?"

"Mom, please," I tried to intervene, but Charlie answered her patiently.

"Angus are primarily beef cattle. Jerseys and Holsteins produce milk."

Fortunately, Charlie had decided not to drink at dinner.

"I heard your horse was lame," my mother continued. "What was wrong with him—or is it her?"

Charlie answered that Dallas was a gelding and that his condition had not been serious. He had had a foot abscess, which the vet drained.

"You wouldn't believe the amount of pus," he said, shaking his head.

"Eww!" Sam and Pete both said, making faces.

"Please, not while we are eating," I said.

"The tricky part was later," Charlie continued, ignoring me, "cleaning the hoof and putting the poultice on his foot. Dallas was having none of it. He nearly took my arm off. It took two of us," Charlie said, nodding toward Cliff.

"Did you read how President Kennedy had pardoned his turkey," I said, to change the subject. "Apparently, he said, 'Let this one grow.'"

"Why did he do that?" Sam asked. "Wasn't he going to have turkey for Thanksgiving?"

"Every year the president of the United States is presented with a live turkey—a Broad Breasted White turkey," my father began. "The ceremony dates back to President Truman and the 1940s. But years earlier, Abraham Lincoln, too, is said to have spared his Thanksgiving turkey, only I think it was a Christmas turkey," my father continued, turning to the twins. "His son Tad, who was ten at the time, loved animals and he had made a pet out of the turkey that was destined for the dinner table, and he begged his father not to kill and eat it.

The boy was so persuasive that President Lincoln agreed to spare the turkey." After a pause, my father added, "Tad had named the turkey Jack."

Cliff hardly said a word during the meal. He left before I brought in the dessert—a pecan and a pumpkin pie and vanilla ice cream—saying that he had promised his son, Alex, that he would be home before his bedtime.

The next day, I drove my parents and the twins to the University of Virginia, to the Rotunda and the Lawn. My father pointed out to Sam and Pete that the Rotunda was modeled on the Pantheon in Rome. Then we walked over to the room Edgar Allan Poe had occupied as a student—West Range number 13. As we peered through the door's iron bars at the narrow bed, the wooden desk, and the two chairs, my father, after clearing his throat, began to recite Poe's famous poem.

For once, the twins listened:

> Once upon a midnight dreary, while I pondered, weak and weary,
> Over many a quaint and curious volume of forgotten lore,—
> While I nodded, nearly napping, suddenly there came a tapping,
> As of some one gently rapping, rapping at my chamber door.
> "'Tis some visitor," I muttered, "tapping at my chamber door;
> Only this and nothing more."

From there, we walked over to the East Gardens—already the twins were climbing on top of the serpentine brick walls and were practicing balancing, while my mother, out of earshot, was calling out to them to be careful and to get down—and I told my father that I was thinking of leaving.

"I think I'll go out west someplace with the twins for a bit," I said. "I've never been and I need to think about things. My marriage," I added, suddenly close to tears.

"I understand," my father said, taking me in his arms.

A serpentine wall, also known as a crinkle crankle wall, can be made just one brick thin. If, for instance, a straight wall, with no buttresses, were to be built with only one brick, it would collapse or topple over.

Soon thereafter, everything—including our lives—unraveled and fell apart very fast. Charlie could not pay off his debts. The mixed Angus-Charolais herd was sold at auction; the bank took over the farm; Charlie's father had a heart attack while playing golf that Charlie's mother blamed on Charlie; Frank and Meryl took Dallas and Esmé and promised to board them indefinitely; Charlie rented a one-bedroom apartment in a condominium near the university—pets were not allowed in the building and he was forced to take Lela and Bella, the English springer spaniels, to a kennel in Keswick, until, he said, he could find a job. A job, maybe, as a farm manager.

To his credit, Charlie did not blame Cliff.

As for me, I hugged Alice Washington goodbye, then, taking Sam and Pete and Nelly, I flew out to California—to as far west as I could go.

Because banks usually insist on personal bonds when making construction loans, developers are much more likely to file for bankruptcy than companies.

Cliff, too, left. He left town without leaving a forwarding address. According to local gossip, he left his wife and son high and dry with almost no support or money. It was also discovered that he had not paid for the maintenance of his plane, nor renewed his registration or license. The Cessna 172 Skyhawk was parked at the airport gathering rust and dust, abandoned. For several days, the good people of Charlottes-ville, outraged by his behavior, talked of little else.

"A no-good thief," "a crook," "he should be horsewhipped" is how they spoke of him.

My guess was that Cliff had gone to Manteo.

Months later—forwarded by Meryl—I received a letter from him:

> It is a cold windy day, the ocean is white with foam, the waves drown out all other noises—if I could just see you, maybe hold you. Hold your slender hand and those long, sensuous fingers. I would be happy just watching you move. You have helped me so many times—out on the ocean riding out a storm, thoughts of you have helped me threw [sic] days and nites of cold, endless seas. I have used you to [illegible]. You are the only one I have ever loved!

"For what is not connected with her to me? and what does not recall her? I cannot look down to this floor, but her features are shaped on the flags! In every cloud, in every tree—filling the air at night, and caught by glimpses in every object, by day I am surrounded with her image!" Heathcliff tells Nelly toward the end of *Wuthering Heights.**

* Brontë, *Wuthering Heights,* pp. 323–34.

The last time we made love—six days exactly before Thanksgiving—on an afternoon that was unseasonably warm for November in Virginia, was again on the plaid blanket in the deserted polo field. On the way home, in the Rover, for some inexplicable reason—we had never done this before—Cliff turned on the radio in the car and that is how we heard the news of President Kennedy's assassination.

Before I got out of the car, Cliff held me in his arms and I began to cry. I don't remember if we said goodbye.

Everyone, I have been told, remembers where they were and what they were doing on that memorable tragic day, and I, too, of course, will remember.

I finished *Wuthering Heights* in California. I read how the novel ends with the death of Heathcliff and how his and Catherine's ghosts continued to roam the Yorkshire moors and haunt the inhabitants.

LABYRINTH TWO

I don't know if there should be a "disclaimer"—the story and title were both inspired and an homage of sorts to Roberto Bolaño, whose story "Labyrinth" (describing a photograph of people sitting around a table in a café) appeared in the New Yorker on January 23, 2012.

I N THE photograph, they are not looking at the camera. They seem unaware that their picture is being taken. Left to right, they are Franco, Eliane, Sergio, and Daphne. The four are sitting around a small round table in the Piazzetta on Capri having drinks—probably drinks before dinner at Gemma's. At Gemma's, they will run into Graham Greene and his companion and great love, Catherine

Walston, who often have dinner there. Sergio, who knows everyone, will walk over to their table to say hello; he will also introduce Franco, Eliane, and Daphne to Graham Greene and Catherine Walston, and Eliane will summon up the courage to tell Graham Greene how much she likes his work—especially, she will say, *The Quiet American*. She might even confess to him how she, too, wants to be a writer. "Good luck then," Graham Greene tells Eliane, giving her a hard, blue-eyed look and a smile that might be both ironic and dismissive. Then turning to Catherine Walston, he says a bit too loudly, "The *spaghetti alle vongole* is reliably good here."

Franco is turned away from the camera and looking at Eliane. One can see only the back of his dark, closely cropped head—except for a small light patch on it that is either a flaw in the photograph or a bald spot. One of Franco's arms is raised, and he is touching his chin in what looks to be an almost feminine gesture; the other arm is resting on his leg, which is crossed. Franco is dressed all in white—white slacks, white shirt—and he gives the impression of being both well groomed and rich. On the arm that is raised, he is wearing a watch. Even if one cannot see Franco's face, his stocky frame gives off an air of solidity and conventionality, although it is, of course, hard to tell what he is thinking as he listens to Eliane speak. And is he really listening to her as he appears to be, or might he instead be trying to imagine what Eliane's breasts look like under her silk blouse since he has noticed that she is not wearing a bra?

Elegantly and sleekly dressed in the silk blouse with a long string of pearls around her neck, Eliane has a cigarette in one hand and, with the other, she is fiddling with the clasp of the gold mesh evening purse on her lap. Her hair is dark and smooth and she looks very pretty. From the way her mouth is open, it is clear that she is speaking, and from the way Sergio is looking at her, it would appear that she is saying something of interest. What could that be? What could a young girl of eighteen or nineteen in Italy in the late 1950s be saying that would command such attention? Something about how Italy was a founding member of the European Economic Community? Or something about Alberto Moravia's latest novel, *La ciociara*, and how it movingly portrays the experience of two women during World War II? Or, more likely, Eliane is telling a story she heard from her father's Jamaican mistress, Francine, about how Orson Welles was giving Prince Dado Ruspoli a lesson in hypnotism while the two men were sitting in a café—a café like this one—and, to show off his occult powers, Orson Welles asked Dado what he would like to see happen next, and Dado said that he would like for the beautiful girl at the next table to spill her drink, a Bloody Mary, down the front of her dress, And guess what, Eliane says. Right then and there, the girl spilled her Bloody Mary all over the front of her dress. However, as Eliane tells this story, she is not looking at either Franco or Sergio but at something or someone else in the café.

"Who was the girl?" Sergio asks.

Still looking away, Eliane shrugs. "I don't know. She was Swedish, I think."

"I don't believe that story," Franco says, shaking his head.

Sergio, who is not Italian but Chilean, is seen in profile. He is dark haired and tanned and has sharp, chiseled features. His face could belong on a Roman coin—a gold coin. He, too, is wearing white—a round-necked polo shirt or light sweater. He stares intently at Eliane as she tells the story of Orson Welles and Prince Ruspoli.

"I know Dado," he also says. "I've seen him walking around Capri with a parrot on his shoulder."

"I heard he's a drug addict," Daphne says, at last joining in the conversation.

Daphne, too, is seen in profile. Her hair, shorter than Eliane's, is dark and curled under in a pageboy; she is pretty in a classical way and is also elegantly dressed in a shirt—it's not clear whether hers is silk or cotton—and white slacks, and she is wearing a pearl necklace, one that circles her neck and does not dangle the way Eliane's does. Her legs outstretched, Daphne is leaning back in her chair as Eliane speaks. Daphne, however, is not looking at Eliane but past her and past Franco. Her look is dreamy or abstracted, as if she is thinking about something else entirely—perhaps about her mother or, more mundanely, about the sandals she plans to buy—or else her look could be the result of her being a bit farsighted.

In fact, her being farsighted is how she and Eliane met. On her hands and knees in the ladies' room of a popular nightclub on the outskirts of Rome called the Belvedere delle Rosa, Daphne was looking for her contact lens that she said had fallen on the floor.

"Here. Is this it?" A glint on the bathroom sink had caught Eliane's eye.

Afterward, Eliane and her date, a college friend on a Fulbright in Italy named Eric, joined Daphne and Daphne's older sister, Shelley, and Shelley's husband, Rob, at their table and watched the floor show, the most memorable act of which was a stripper who at the last possible moment—taking off her bra—turned out to be a man.

"I knew it all the time," Eric said.

"I didn't," Eliane said. In spite of herself, she was shocked.

In the taxi, on the way back to her father's apartment, Eric kissed Eliane, and although she was not attracted to him, she let him put his tongue in her mouth. Once home, she rinsed out her mouth.

As it turned out, Eliane and Daphne were both spending the summer in Rome with their fathers. Eliane's father, who is French and not Italian and divorced from Eliane's mother, is a film producer and, like many of his confreres, came to "Hollywood on the Tiber" after the war to make movies. Daphne's father is an American and a widower; he lives in Rome because he is a homosexual. He shares his apartment on Via della Croce off Piazza di Spagna with a man named Marco. Although Daphne had mentioned Marco from time to time—he is younger than her father, good-looking, and he teaches law at Sapienza University of Rome—Eliane, as yet, had not met Marco and did not press Daphne about him or about her father, although she would have liked to. Eliane was curious, as Daphne's father is the first openly homosexual man—commonly referred to as a "pansy"—she had met, and as far as she was concerned, Daphne's father did not look or act differently from anyone else.

Capri was Franco's idea. Franco is from Milan, where he works at his family's company. He and Sergio had run into each other earlier that summer at a lighting manufacturers' convention in Turin—Sergio, among other things, represents a Murano glassblower—and Sergio had complained to Franco about how hot Rome was in the summer and how everyone he knew had gone elsewhere—to Forte dei Marmi or to Porto Ercole—and that was when Franco suggested he come to Capri for a few days.

"Bring a friend—a woman—if you like," Franco had also said.

"I'll bring two. One for you," Sergio replied.

This is Eliane and Daphne's first visit to Capri. It is an adventure for them, perhaps a romantic adventure. And, to convince their fathers to let them go, they told a lie.

"Daphne's father?" Eliane's father had remarked, raising his eyebrows. "The pansy"—only he used the French expression *tapette*—"is inviting you to Capri?"

"Lucky you," Francine said, and, being practical, she had insisted on taking Eliane shopping for a new bathing suit—a bikini to replace her one-piece. "You're young, you have a nice body—what have you got to hide?" Francine had said to her.

"The producer?" Daphne's father, in turn, asked. "Maybe you'll see a lot of movie stars."

"Greta Garbo goes to Capri," Marco said, "only no one ever sees her there."

Franco's parents, who are sailing on their yacht in the Mediterranean for two weeks, have a villa in Capri. The villa is a ten-minute picturesque walk from the Piazzetta along winding alleys flanked with bougainvillea and oleander bushes and high stone walls topped with broken glass. It has a swimming pool and a large terrace with a magnificent view of the ocean and the Faraglioni—the Italian term for "stacks"—all three of which have individual names: Stella, Mezzo, and Scopolo. The villa itself is reached by climbing forty-four steep stone steps. The rooms are airy and unpretentiously furnished with brightly upholstered rattan and wicker; the floors are made up of individually fired ceramic tiles known as *le riggiole*; plain white cotton curtains billow out gracefully in the breeze from the open windows in the bedroom Eliane and Daphne share.

On their way to the Piazzetta to have a drink before dinner with Franco and Sergio, who had already left the villa on an errand of their own, Eliane and Daphne stopped in front of Amedeo Canfora's shop—the shoemaker to Princess Margaret, Maria Callas, and Sophia Loren, among others—and watched as he wove and nailed strips of colorful leather to make a sandal.

"*Torneremo domani,*" Daphne told Amedeo, catching his eye.

"*Farò un bel paio specialmente per voi, signorina,*" he answered Daphne, smiling.

"You've made your first conquest in Capri," Eliane told Daphne as they started to walk toward the Piazzetta again.

Both girls laughed.

Actually, they will make a few more conquests at the nightclub across from the Grand Hotel Quisisana, where the four go dancing after they have had dinner at Gemma's. The nightclub is in the basement and crowded; a live band plays mostly South American music—sambas, rumbas, and a lot of cha-cha-chas.

Cha-cha-cha—as soon as Eliane and Daphne start to sit down after dancing with Franco and Sergio, someone else comes up to their table to ask one of them to dance.

"*Permesso?*" he says.

"*Paolo,*" he also says, introducing himself.

Cha-cha-cha.

Despite his solid build, Franco will turn out to be a good dancer. He holds Eliane tightly in his arms, thus verifying for himself that she is not wearing a bra. He would like to sleep with her, but he is afraid that she prefers Sergio to him, and except for dancing with him now, Eliane has pretty much ignored him all evening. During dinner, her remarks were mostly addressed to Sergio—asking questions about the glassblower from Murano, asking him who else he represented, and asking questions Franco thought were indiscreet. Perhaps she had had too much wine—they had drunk two bottles of Falanghina, the local white wine—but hard to tell since he did not know her and perhaps, too, American girls were different from Italian girls. Less modest. More aggressive. Daphne is quiet; he likes her although she is not as pretty—no, not as sexy as Eliane. And—Franco cannot keep himself from having this thought—Daphne is wearing a bra.

Daphne's mother died exactly a year ago after a long battle with ovarian cancer. Away at school, Daphne saw her mother only during the holidays, and each time she came home from Connecticut to Houston, where the family lived, her mother was significantly worse and each time, too, although she felt tremendously guilty about leaving again, Daphne was also tremendously relieved to go. Several years older, her sister, Shelley, was already married and she, too, had left Houston and was living in Boston with her husband, Rob, and as a result, Daphne, as often as she could, went to stay with Shelley in Boston instead of going back home. When her mother finally died, Daphne went back to Houston for the funeral and for what would turn out to be the last time, as it was shortly afterward that her father announced to his daughters that he was retiring from his law practice and that he was in love with an Italian man he had met at a conference and would be moving to Rome. Except for staying with her sister in Boston, Daphne is pretty much homeless.

"What sort of company does your family own?" Eliane asks Franco, in an effort to free herself on the dance floor from his tight embrace—so tight she can feel his erection.

"We make electric equipment and magnetos—"

"Magnetos? What are they for?"

"Magnetos are used in the ignition system of spark-ignition piston engines like those in small aircrafts, motor-cycles, electric lawn mowers, chain saws—"

"And where did you learn to speak English?" Eliane does not let Franco finish.

Instead of answering Eliane, he squeezes her to him again.

Franco's English is an anglicized English. He spent a year at Harrow and later went to the London School of Economics, which he refers to as LSE. He deeply resents that people—Americans especially—assume that he is an ignorant "wop." *How many languages do you speak,* he wants to ask Eliane, *aside from your bad Italian?* He is starting to regret that he has invited Sergio and the two American girls—although he did not officially invite them, Sergio did—for the weekend. He likes Sergio well enough, but Eliane and Daphne strike him as young and naive. He wonders if they are virgins. *Probably,* he thinks.

Cha-cha-cha.

How do you know Sergio? Eliane wants to ask after a while but does not.

Sergio, too, is a good dancer, albeit a different sort of dancer. He holds Eliane lightly; his hand on her lower back exerts just the right amount of pressure for her to follow him.

"You're a good dancer," he tells her.

"No, you are the one who is a good dancer," Eliane says. Sergio shakes his head and laughs.

"You know, you remind me a little of my wife—the same hair," he says, smiling and moving his hand lower, almost onto Eliane's buttocks.

"Your wife?" Eliane asks, pulling back a little.

"My ex-wife, Cosetta," Sergio says. "But we were married for only a few months."

"Oh. What happened?" Eliane can't help asking him.

"Cosetta met someone else," Sergio replies with a sigh.

"So you got divorced?"

"No, you can't get a divorce in Italy. We had the marriage annulled."

Sergio pulls Eliane to him, and for a few minutes and until the music stops, they dance with their bodies pressed together.

Daphne introduced Sergio to Eliane. Sergio, Daphne said, had done some work for her father—finding him the apartment on Via della Croce, then putting him in touch with an electrician, a plumber, a decorator. Daphne laughed and said,

"Sergio knows everyone, and the funny thing is that he is not even from Rome; he is not even Italian."

At dinner at Gemma's that night, Eliane, emboldened perhaps by all the wine, asks Sergio, "Why did you leave Chile?"

"It's a long story," Sergio answers. "I was young, a teenager, and I got involved with a group of men who were Communists. Gabriel González Videla, who was president of Chile at the time, first expelled the Communists from his cabinet, then he passed a law, Ley de Defensa Permanente de la Democracia, that banned the Communist Party. He did this mainly to gain the economic support of the United States." Sergio stops a moment and gives Eliane a meaningful look. "Which he got. Then," he resumes, "a lot of Communists were arrested and many people, including Pablo Neruda, fled Chile. I fled as well."

No one says anything for a moment, then Franco raises his glass and says, "To Sergio and to Pablo Neruda." After another pause, he also says, "Falanghina is an ancient Greek grape that prospers in this porous volcanic soil full of minerals such as olivine, pyroxene, amphibole—"

"Franco is showing off again," Sergio says, interrupting him.

"I love the wine," Daphne says quickly.

It is not clear to her or to Eliane, for that matter—although neither one of them has discussed this—what is expected of them on this weekend in Capri. Not only are they staying in

Franco's parents' villa, but it also seems that so far Franco is paying for everything—their drinks on the Piazzetta, the dinner at Gemma's. Tomorrow, he says, he will take them down to Gracie Fields's establishment, the Canzone del Mare, for lunch and to swim. In addition, Franco has talked about renting a motorboat and going around the island and visiting the Blue Grotto.

"Or we could climb up to Tiberius's villa," Sergio, who has been to Capri before, suggests.

Franco shakes his head. "Too hot to walk all the way up there," he says, "and anyway, there isn't much to see anymore. A pile of roofless buildings and a few columns left standing."

"Still, it's impressive," Sergio argues. "The three-hundred-meter drop to the sea—the Salto di Tiberio, where Tiberius threw the people he did not like to their deaths."

"He was crazy," Franco says, "and a pervert. He trained young boys to swim alongside him and bite at his private parts."

"Gross," Eliane says.

Eliane much prefers Sergio to Franco. Sergio, she thinks, is intelligent and sensitive. Also, he has had an interesting life and has had to make it on his own, while Franco, she thinks, is rich and spoiled. She did not like the way he was looking at her in the café on the Piazzetta, as if he could see her undressed. She wonders, too, what Daphne thinks of Franco. Daphne is less opinionated than she is, less critical. Maybe Daphne likes Franco. *Well, she can have him,* Eliane thinks. As for her, she likes a different type of man. A man like Sergio or a man like the darkly handsome waiter she saw at the Piazzetta tonight. Never mind that he probably knows how handsome he is and that he preys on the women tourists. A lot of the customers seemed to know him by name. "Marcello!" they called out to him. "Marcello!"

"Si, si, subito, signor," Marcello replied good-naturedly, at the same time that he appeared oblivious to their demands.

When Franco had gotten ready to pay, he had motioned to Marcello, who this time came over to their table right away. As Marcello made change, he looked directly at Eliane and softly began to sing a song popular that summer:

Tu sei per me la più bella del mondo . . .

Eliane remembers blushing.

"All Italian waiters are born singers and liars," Franco said, as he left Marcello a tip. "It's in their blood. Come, let's eat. I'm hungry."

Remembering what Graham Greene told Catherine Walston, Eliane orders the *spaghetti alle vongole* at Gemma's. Daphne orders *spaghetti carbonara*, saying she is allergic to shellfish.

She also says, "I know mussels aren't crustaceans, but I don't want to take a chance."

"No, of course not," Sergio says, frowning. "My friend Gianni, the glassblower in Murano I told you about, nearly died from eating something. Nuts, I think—his throat closed and he could not breathe."

"Anaphylactic shock," Daphne says.

"Thank God he didn't die," Franco says. "Gianni is a very talented glassblower. He is one of the few who still uses a special glass-forging technique developed in the seventeenth century that amplifies . . ."

Instead of paying attention as Franco talks about old-fashioned glassblowing techniques, Eliane finds herself thinking about the handsome waiter, Marcello. She knows it is totally inappropriate and that they have nothing in common, and yet she is attracted to him. She fantasizes about making love to Marcello.

She is sunbathing in her new blue-and-white-striped bikini, and Marcello comes and sits down next to her on the beach. His body is lean, hairless, and brown. He is wearing faded black cotton trunks.

"Shall we go for a swim?" he asks her in Italian.

"Si," Eliane replies.

They swim far out to where the turquoise sea turns to a darker navy blue—both are strong swimmers. Occasionally, Eliane feels Marcello's arm or leg brush against her in the water. Once back on the beach, laughing, Marcello holds out his hand and helps her to climb onto a secluded flat rock. Together they lie next to each other in the sun.

"Bellina," he says, as he leans over and is about to kiss her.

"You've seen the chandelier, haven't you, Eli?" Daphne is saying to her. "In my Dad's dining room. Gianni, Sergio's friend, made it especially for him."

Graham Greene and Catherine Walston have gotten up from their table and are getting ready to leave. As they walk past, Graham Greene pats Sergio on the shoulder and says something to him about catching the last bus.

"He lives in Anacapri," Sergio explains.

"We should go," Franco says. "Anacapri is beautiful and much quieter than Capri. Axel Munthe lived in Anacapri. My parents knew him well. He had a beautiful villa—Villa San Michele—filled with fragments of sarcophaguses and Roman busts. And dogs." Franco gives a laugh. "My parents said that each time they went at least a dozen dogs were running around the villa. All kinds of dogs—strays mostly. Munthe loved animals. He created a bird sanctuary in Anacapri."

"I'd like to go," Daphne says. "I love dogs."

In fact, once she goes back to the States, Daphne plans on getting a dog—a dog from the SPCA, a dog who needs a home. Her father, she knows, would disapprove; he does not like dogs. He claims that they are dirty and that they shed. He is excessively tidy and insists on everything in his apartment being kept in its place—the sofa cushions plumped up—and is irritated if Daphne leaves a glass or one of her magazines on the coffee table. He was like that in the house in Houston but in Rome it is worse. Marco teases him and says he acts like a *pignola vecchia*, and Daphne is grateful to Marco for this. Mostly, in the apartment with her father, she hardly dares breathe.

Before they leave Gemma's to go to the nightclub across from the Grand Hotel Quisisana, Eliane and Daphne excuse themselves from the table and go to the ladies' room. Once inside, they find the *toilette* occupied.

"I like Sergio," Eliane starts to tell Daphne as they stand in front of the bathroom sink, waiting.

"He's nice," Daphne agrees.

"You're not in love with him, are you?" Eliane asks.

"Oh, no. Impossible—" Daphne starts to say, when the door to the *toilette* opens and Catherine Walston walks out.

"I never know how long that old bus is going to take," Catherine Walston says with a smile as she sidesteps around Eliane and Daphne to wash her hands at the sink.

"Go ahead," Daphne then says to Eliane, "I can wait."

Eliane does not mind that each summer when she goes to visit her father in Italy, he has a mistress. On the contrary, she is relieved—relieved for two reasons. The first is that until this summer when she met Daphne, she has known no one her own age in Rome, and the mistress, whoever she is, becomes a sort of companion for Eliane. They meet during the day, go to the beach, shop together. The second reason is that Eliane and her father are awkward with each other. Unused to her presence, Eliane's father does not know what to do or what to say to her; also, he is very critical at times, even harsh. The mistress takes the pressure off Eliane; Eliane is no longer the sole object of her father's attention or, for that matter, his affection. And she likes Francine. In addition to being glamorous and an actress—Francine played a slave in *Quo Vadis*—she is friendly and candid.

"What part of Jamaica are you from?" Eliane had asked her.

"Mandeville, which is quite different from the rest of Jamaica," Francine answered. "It's not on the coast but inland on a plateau. If you were to go there, you'd think you were in an English village. There's a town green, a church, a courthouse, a library, and all the names are English: Battersea, Knockpatrick, Clover, Waltham . . ." Francine gave a laugh. "A time warp."

"And why did you leave Jamaica?" Eliane had also asked.

"As a teenager—I was around your age, maybe a little younger—I was bored and I did not want to go to school, so I would hitch a ride to the beach at Negril, and one day a French photographer saw me and took my picture. He told me I could be a model. I believed him and I left Jamaica."

"Would you go back?"

"All these questions," Francine said. Then, after pausing a moment, she said, "There's an old Jamaican saying that goes, 'Talk and taste your tongue,' which means 'think before you speak.' I know you mean well and that you are a nice, intelligent girl, but, to tell the truth, talking about Jamaica breaks my heart."

It is two o'clock in the morning when they leave the night-club across from the Hotel Quisisana and start to walk back to Franco's parents' villa. Franco and Daphne are walking up ahead, and Franco has his arm around Daphne's waist. He looks as if he is holding her up. Going up the steps from the night-club, Daphne had missed a step, fallen, and twisted her ankle.

"It's these shoes," she complains. "Tomorrow I'm going to buy some sandals," she says. "Gold sandals," she adds. Daphne sounds a little drunk.

Sergio and Eliane are walking behind them.

"A beautiful night," Eliane says, looking up at the sky.

"Careful," Sergio tells her. "Look where you're going—not like Daphne."

Eliane does not answer. Her arms hang limply by her sides, and she wishes that Sergio would take her hand.

"I've never seen so many stars," she says.

"There's no moon, that's why," Sergio answers. "We should have brought along a flashlight. The streets are dark."

Eliane says nothing.

Up ahead, she hears Daphne laughing.

Marcello, she thinks, would have his arms around her.

"What about your parents?" Eliane asks Sergio. "Are they still in Chile?"

"My mother is," Sergio answers.

And your father? but Eliane does not dare press him further.

Up the forty-four steep steps, Eliane counts them under her breath.

"Do you think Franco carried Daphne up all these steps," Sergio says with a laugh. "I don't see them."

When they reach the terrace, Eliane says, "I'm going to sit outside for a few minutes and look at the stars."

"I'll join you," Sergio says, then adds, "Do you want something to drink? I'll go see what there is."

When he comes back, he holds two glasses of beer. "I couldn't find any of that old Greek wine," he tells Eliane, handing her a glass before he pulls up a chaise longue and sits down next to her.

"Beer is good," Eliane says.

"I'm looking for a shooting star," she also tells Sergio. "Then I'll make a wish."

"What will you wish for?" he asks.

"I don't know, but if I tell you it won't come true."

Sergio does not say anything.

"How do you know Franco?" Eliane finally asks.

"Through Marco," Sergio answers.

"Daphne's father's Marco?"

"Before he started teaching at Sapienza, Marco represented Franco's company in a suit, and at the time, Marco and I were . . ." Sergio pauses.

Eliane's heart starts to beat rapidly.

". . . friends," Sergio says softly.

In the room she shares with Daphne, Eliane turns out the light and gets into bed. Next to hers, Daphne's bed is empty. Shutting her eyes, Eliane tries to think about Marcello and how they are lying next to each other in their bathing suits on the flat rock and how Marcello leans over and is about to kiss her.

In the photograph, the four glasses and the bottle on top of the round table in the café on the Piazzetta are empty, and soon Franco will signal to the handsome waiter, pay the bill, and the four of them will get up and go to dinner at Gemma's, where they will meet Graham Greene and Catherine Walston.

THE DEAD SWAN

Iᴛ's ᴀ cold, windy early spring day and Sadie is walking by herself along the beach and probably not looking down or at where she is going, so she nearly trips over it—the dead swan—only she doesn't right away recognize what it is. She stops and stares at it, and because she is unhappy she thinks it is beautiful. She picks up the dead swan in her arms and walks home with it.

What does a swan weigh—twenty? Twenty-five pounds?

Her husband, Mason, is away—he is away in jail awaiting his trial—otherwise she would not have brought the swan home. Sadie can hear what he would have to say to her about it:

Christ! Sadie, get that damn bird out of here.

Or, more threatening:

Get rid of that fucking bird before I—

If he was high, which he usually was now, he might have raised his hand at her. A couple of times already he had swung and missed. Mason is not as coordinated or as strong as he used to be. The drugs, Sadie guesses, part of the reason he is now in jail.

Mason has been diagnosed as bipolar and a bunch of other things that Sadie can't remember offhand. Manic depressive was one of them. He was on meds, but half the time he refused to take them. Mason said that the meds made him feel slow and stupid and gave him a dry mouth. *I can't even get it up anymore*, Mason had complained, making a sound that was meant to be a laugh but wasn't.

Holding the swan like a baby, Sadie places it gently on the old-fashioned canvas swing chair in the screened-in porch, careful not to rock it. She spreads out one of his great wings—three feet?—then the other. She runs her hand down the swan's gray legs. No breaks—last year she saw a one-legged seagull hopping pitifully on the beach—and no dried blood. She feels along his rough, dark-orange beak to the little black basal knob. The swan's head and long neck are resting on his breast as if he were asleep and he appears perfect. Carefully, Sadie sits down next to him. *He*, she thinks, but perhaps the swan is female, a she. Impossible to tell about birds unless she was to examine the vent area, which she is not going to do.

Sadie works as a substitute teacher at the local elementary school. From one day to the next, with no preparation until she arrives at the school and is assigned her class, she can be teaching third graders about the Lewis and Clark expedition or sixth graders algebra or, as she did last Monday, Greek myths to fifth graders. They had discussed all the gods: Zeus, Athena, Apollo, Aphrodite—their traditional roles and their deeds, but not, as she suddenly thinks now, their misdeeds— transmogrified into a swan, Zeus the rapist.

At least, Sadie thinks, Mason couldn't rape anyone.

Instead he took off all his clothes in a playground full of children. Sadie does not want to imagine the scene, but can: terrified kids, screaming parents, a rush of security guards, then police. Fortunately—if there is anything fortunate about this—Mason's disrobing occurred in a different state and so far the school where Sadie substitutes has not gotten wind of the incident. Otherwise—otherwise, she might be dismissed.

Mason is not always crazy. Sadie remembers how a few days before the incident in the playground, they went to the local pound to adopt a dog. Immediately Sadie had fallen in love with a little brindle terrier mix, but Mason, in his reasonable voice, said that a dog was a big responsibility and they should think it over. He also said that Sadie was too impetuous, too quick to form judgments. Afterward, they had gone to the only decent restaurant in town and she, Sadie remembers, had the swordfish and Mason had the hanger steak. They also drank a bottle of wine, and he made her laugh by wiggling his ears—first the right one, then the left—and promising to show her how. Later that night, Mason tried to make love.

* * *

A month ago when Mason was first jailed, Sadie had gotten up at four in the morning in order to arrive at the detention center on time for visiting hours. Although she was early, the line of visitors—most of whom were either black or Hispanic —was already long and she had to wait, standing, for over an hour outside in the cold. First her purse was searched and her bottle of Valium was confiscated and thrown into a trash bin, then she was told to remove her shoes, her jewelry—a simple gold chain and her wedding ring—which, along with her purse, she had to put inside a locker for safekeeping. Sadie then went through a metal detector and was body-searched by a policewoman. The policewoman felt her bra for wire and put her hand inside Sadie's underpants. Finally, she was taken to a large room where several prisoners and their families were already sitting around small tables, and Mason was brought in. Mason was wearing an orange jumpsuit and his hair was cut short. He had stitches over one eye and it took a moment for Sadie to know what to say to him.

"What happened to your eye?" she finally asked.

Mason shrugged as he sat down across from Sadie.

"No physical contact," the guard warned her.

"Are you okay?" Sadie continued.

Again, Mason said nothing.

"Can you wiggle your ears?" Sadie said in an effort to make him smile. "I've been practicing just the way you said by just going through the motions in my head thinking what it would be—"

Cutting her off, Mason stood up so abruptly that he knocked over his chair and yelled, "Jesus! I don't believe you, Sadie!"

A guard came over. "Keep it down," he told Mason.

"The hell I am going to keep it down." Mason was still yelling as he pushed past the table between him and Sadie.

The guard grabbed Mason just in time and started to take him away.

"You know what," Mason shouted back at Sadie before the door shut behind him, "you're a fucking idiot and an evil cunt."

In front of the bathroom mirror that night, Sadie, in vain, tried to wiggle her ears; instead she burst into tears.

The swan's eyes are closed and Sadie is smoothing his feathers. She has read that swans can be very aggressive, especially if they have a nest nearby. Flapping their huge wings and hissing, they will chase away predators—human predators as well. Once, a Japanese photographer who wanted to take a picture of a nest got too close and was killed by a swan. How? Sadie can't help wondering. Was he beaten to death by the swan's powerful wings? And how, she wonders, was his death explained to his wife and his children? Killer swan. However, this swan, her swan, looks peaceful.

* * *

Secretly, Sadie was relieved that Mason could not get it up anymore, although she would of course never tell Mason or anyone else for that matter. Recently, sex had been rough and unsatisfying. Scary, really, and more like Mason was some stranger she had met on one of those internet dating sites. A really crazy person who might urinate on her or hack her to pieces.

What, she wonders, does swan meat taste like? Probably like goose. For one Thanksgiving dinner, Sadie had eaten the goose Mason had shot and cooked, and although she told him the goose was delicious, privately, she had disliked the tough and gamy taste. In England, in the olden days—she remembers reading somewhere—only royalty, kings and queens, were allowed to eat swans. They still are, only they don't.

The other fact Sadie knows about swans—a fact everyone knows—is that swans are monogamous and that they mate for life. Not so, she thinks, about herself and Mason.

Ron Shirer, the math teacher at the school, who seems like a nice guy and is single, has asked her out for a cup of coffee, and as yet she hasn't taken him up on it.

"I'll go for coffee," she bends her head to tell the swan. "Maybe I'll go for more than coffee," she says, giving a little laugh.

When Sadie was young she took ballet. For a while she fantasized that she would become a dancer—a principal dancer in a company like the Bolshoi or ABT. She would be famous and she would travel. She was a good dancer. She had the body for it and a great turnout—Alicia, her teacher with the fake Russian name, had told her so.

Ta da dum, ta da dum, Sadie hums the first few bars of *Swan Lake* and is tempted to get up and dance. She regrets it now. She should have persevered. After ballet, she decided to become a vet, but she hated the college biology courses and gave that up, too. Next she took up photography—she was told she had a good eye—and she managed to buy a secondhand Rolleiflex 3.5 F, her prize possession, that had cost her; she also managed to get one of her black-and-white photographs—a flock of starlings perched on a power line—in a group show, which was where she met Mason. They were going to start a bed-and-breakfast; instead, they went into debt renovating the house and Mason started to deal in illegal substances and she got a job substitute teaching.

Maybe, Sadie thinks, if she kisses the swan, the swan will turn into a handsome prince. Or, if not a real prince, into a handsome young man with whom she will live happily ever after.

Inside the house the phone rings. Sadie does not move; she lets the voice mail pick up.

"Hey, Sadie," she hears Mason say. "Good news. They're letting me out on probation next Wednesday. Can you come pick me up and bring me some clothes? A pair of khakis and my jacket—the jacket is at the cleaners. I love you, baby."

The cleaners is next door to the pound and Sadie wonders if the little brindle terrier mix she liked so much is still available for adoption—probably not.

Time to go in, Sadie tells herself, feeling cold all of a sudden. Tomorrow she will take the swan back to the beach. And, if it's a nice day, she also tells herself, she will bring along her camera—it's been ages since she has taken any photographs. She gives the swan a little pat and stands up, then hesitates, not wanting to leave him out on the porch alone. In the fading evening light, his shape becomes more and more indistinct. Soon all Sadie can see is the silvery gleam of his feathers. In the night's approaching lonely darkness, she wonders about the swan's forlorn mate.

Upstairs in the bedroom, Sadie looks on the top shelf of her closet, behind the boxes of old sweaters, scarves, and hats, where she hides the camera, but the Rolleiflex is not there.

The fucking bastard!

Mason must have taken it and sold it. Still, she can hardly believe that he could have done that and, to make sure, she sweeps all the contents off the shelf—the boxes of sweaters, scarves, and hats—onto the floor.

Afterward, Sadie rummages through the bedside table drawers looking for where Mason keeps pills—Ambien,

Percodan, oxycodone—anything that will let her sleep. She takes two of the pink pills and goes to bed.

When Sadie wakes up the next morning it is already noon. Quickly, she puts on her sweatpants and a T-shirt—she has no memory of getting undressed and, briefly, she wonders if she ate supper. In the kitchen, she starts up the coffee machine before going out to the screened-in porch. The porch door is wide open and the canvas swing chair is creaking slightly. The swan, of course, is gone.

CARL SCHURZ PARK

THE BOYS—there were four and they were not entirely sober—carried off the girl on their shoulders. All of them were yelling—the boys and the girl, too. The girl was yelling in panic. This was not a joke. She was black and maybe fifteen or sixteen years old. Her skirt had hiked up, exposing her pink panties that had TUESDAY stitched on the back, only it wasn't Tuesday; it was Saturday.

"If you don't stop hollering," one of the boys said, "we'll throw you in the river."

Which is what they did. Up on the esplanade and over the rail she went and into the East River. The girl did not know how to swim, and even if she had known how, the water was cold and the current was strong.

It was night and they were in Carl Schurz Park, off East End Avenue in New York City.

The girl—she had said her name was Petra although it wasn't, and anyway, it didn't matter because none of the four boys called her by it—was high; the boys had picked her up at Penn Station and promised her cash. The boys—all of them were white and all of them seniors at a private school in the city. Justin drove his father's Volvo station wagon up Sixth Avenue, then through Central Park—which, unusually, was open to traffic—and Alan shouted out the open car window as they passed a horse and carriage.

"Assholes!"

Justin laughed and the car swerved.

They drove to the Ninetieth Street exit, then down Fifth Avenue to Eighty-Sixth Street toward East End Avenue. They were drinking from a bottle of Stoli vodka.

They were going to fuck the girl. Earlier Justin had said he had never fucked a black girl before—the others said they hadn't either. Justin also said he wanted to see if it felt different. The others said, "Yeah, right."

In the back seat, Aaron handed the girl the vodka and she took a swig, then, gagging, she spat it out.

"Bitch," Peter said.

"Careful or this bottle is going to go straight up your ass," he told her.

The girl laughed. "Fuck you," she said.

"No, fuck you," Aaron said.

"I have to pee," the girl all of a sudden said.

"Wait, you can pee in the park," Aaron said.

"My parents used to live in this neighborhood, and as a kid, I used to walk our dog there," Alan said from the front seat.

"What kind of a dog?" Peter asked.

"A cocker spaniel."

"Did you have to pick up his shit?"

"Her shit. No, I just left it. Ha ha," Alan also said, then added, "Her name was Coco."

"Shit, shit, shit," said the girl.

"Oh, Christ," Peter said, "she's peeing right here on the seat."

"Oh, fuck," Justin said, half turning around—they were on Eighty-Sixth Street between Lexington and Third Avenue; in back of them a car honked. "What the fuck am I supposed to do? It's my father's damn car! And shut the fuck up!" he yelled at the car in back of him, giving the driver the finger.

"Pull over," Alan yelled.

"I can't," Justin said.

"I don't feel good," the girl said.

"Oh, Christ, she's going to be sick now," Aaron said.

"Open the car door!" Justin yelled. "Throw her out."

"No!" the girl screamed.

The light was green and Justin gunned the Volvo down the street toward East End Avenue and Carl Schurz Park.

Swept along on her back by the current, her skirt spread out on either side of her like sails in the water, she felt clear for the first time in a long time. The shock of the cold water, she thought, but she was not afraid. She kept her arms by her side and did not move. Tilting her chin, she looked up at the sky—too dark for stars and too many lights across on the shore of Roosevelt Island. In the distance, a big Pepsi-Cola sign blinked red, and she remembered the story she had heard about how in India—or maybe it was in Africa, she could not be sure—Pepsi-Cola was assumed to be the plural for Coca-Cola. She thought about how good it might be to drink a Coke right now. She also thought about her older brother, Kim, and how he had this trick—although it was more like an ability than a trick. He could open his throat and drink a whole bottle of Coke without ever once swallowing. He could do that with a can of beer, too. A Bud. A couple of times, she had tried, but she never could achieve it. She always had to swallow. She wondered vaguely about Kim and his girlfriend, Doreen, and what they were doing right this minute and whether they would miss her. Would anyone miss her? she wondered, but she did not want to think about that. She wanted to think about drinking a Coke and about how good it would taste. She opened her mouth a little and let the river water in.

Once, at school, in the hall and in between classes, Alan tried to go up to Justin and say something, but Justin would not let him and said, "It never happened, is that clear? And if you ever say anything I'll fucking kill you."

Who the hell was Carl Schurz anyway? And what bearing does *he* have on this story? None really. A German immigrant, he came to America in 1852 at the age of twenty-three, and despite having fought for the Union at Gettysburg—a bullet pierced the thick part of his horse's neck, underneath the mane, killing it, but Schurz was unharmed—and despite having had an impressive political career, Carl Schurz's accomplishments and life have faded into near obscurity.

For sure not one of the four boys who threw the girl into the East River knew anything about him, not even the slightest detail like the bullet that pierced his horse's neck at Gettysburg—nor would they ever. Nor would Alan, who, as a boy, had taken Coco to the park so often that he claimed he knew it like the back of his hand and could walk through it with his eyes fucking shut. *Ha ha.* Only years later, when he was living across the river in Brooklyn and married with his first child on the way, and while he was having dinner with friends at a Japanese restaurant and he had—a propos of nothing in particular—happened to have mentioned that he had once lived near the park, did the name Carl Schurz come up again.

"You don't know the story?" Alan's friend had asked. "I can't remember who told it to me, but apparently there is a Peter Pan statue in Carl Schurz Park—do you remember it?"

"Yeah, sort of. It was off to one side of the park, I think," Alan answered.

"Well, one night, years ago, some vandals removed it and threw the statue into the East River but, miraculously, the New York Police Department found it on the bottom and dredged it up. The statue was restored and eventually returned to the park."

"That's amazing that they found it," Alan's wife said. "You never heard that story, Alan?" she asked.

Alan shook his head, all at once recalling how one afternoon Coco had left a mess of yellow liquid diarrhea laced with strings of bloody mucus in the grass at the base of the statue, and he felt a moment of overpowering discomfort that manifested itself as nausea and a lack of focus that he could neither understand nor place but that he told himself must be because of the almost visceral memory of the shit.

"I love Peter Pan," Alan's wife was saying. "The story, I mean. And, Alan," she added, "someday you will have to take me to that park."

A Natural State

My name is Yon Yonson,
I live in Wisconsin.
I work in a lumber yard there.
The people I meet as
I walk down the street,
They say "Hello!"
I say "Hello!"
They say "What's your name."
I say: My name is Yon Yonson . . .

The absurd jingle replays in her head. *My name is Yon Yonson,*
I live in Wisconsin . . . What is the guy's name?

Yann something.

In the last few hours, he has sent her dozens of emails.
Crazy. He must be crazy. He writes that he is Swedish.

You don't know me, Claire, but I know you. I know all about you.
About your time as a Rajneeshee. 14. jan. 2018 kl. 11:16 skrev Yann
Johansen <yjohansen@icloud.com>

Despite their blond good looks, there are a lot of crazy people in Sweden, she thinks. And a lot of crime as well.

She thinks of Kenneth Branagh, who is not Swedish but who plays Wallander, the Swedish detective who, once a week, solves one grisly murder after the other. Then there are the novels of Joe Nesbø, featuring the shrewd alcoholic Harry Hole, and those of Peter Høeg, introducing nervy, sardonic Smilla Jaspersen, which describe in lurid detail how all those beautiful Swedes are getting decapitated, dismembered, disemboweled . . .

Is it the darkness? she wonders. The lack of sun?

In real life, too. The man who gunned down a bunch of kids who were camping on that island—what was his name?

Anders Behring Breivik.

Yann Johansen is the emailer's name, and in another email to her, he quotes Adi Shankara:

"All the manifested world of things and beings are projected by imagination upon the substratum which is the Eternal All-pervading Vishnu, whose nature is Existence-Intelligent; just as the different ornaments are all made out of the same gold." 14. jan. 2018 kl. 11:20 skrev Yann Johansen <yjohansen@icloud.com>

Quickly followed by another email saying he knew she had been a follower of Bhagwan.

Then another:

Believe me, Claire, I am the real thing. My body is functioning in a perfect natural way. Not like your phony Bhagwan. 14. jan. 2018 kl. 11:25 skrev Yann Johansen <yjohansen@icloud.com>

Still another:

He's the crazy one, Claire. 14. jan. 2018 kl. 11:28 skrev Yann Johansen <yjohansen@icloud.com>.

How, she wondered, had he found her?

A long time ago—thirty-four years to be exact—she had posted online an account of her time as a Rajneeshee. This Yann person must have found it and read it.

Did you sleep with Bhagwan? Truth is important. Isn't that what he told you? Did you sleep with him? 14. jan. 2018 kl. 11:34 skrev Yann Johansen <yjohansen@icloud.com>

Of course, she won't answer him.

My name is Yon Yonson, I live in Wisconsin . . .

She and Pete, her boyfriend at the time, backpacked in India for several months, and, always, they ran into the same people, also backpacking, in youth hostels, on buses and trains: Brits, Australians, a handsome French couple—Anouk and Philippe. She will never forget them—how intrepid they were. And they were the ones who suggested they go to Poona.

To the ashram.

You must have been a good-looking young girl. A sexy-looking girl in your red dress. Or did you wear red pants? Ha ha. 14. jan. 2018 kl. 11:41 skrev Yann Johansen <yjohansen@icloud.com>

In Poona, Pete got dysentery. It got so bad that he couldn't stop shitting—a painful yellow stream. The doctor in the ashram started out by giving him herbal medicines—teas, infusions—but they didn't work. He then tried giving him other stuff—Claire is not sure what—drugs of some kind, but those only made Pete feel worse. He said he felt like he was going out of his head.

Then, too, Pete had started to cry. Cry like a baby. She had felt sorry for him but she also had started to dislike him—hate him, actually. It was so unseemly. Eventually, Pete left and went back home. Relieved, Claire stayed on in Poona with Anouk and Philippe.

Claire did sleep with Philippe. She slept with Anouk as well. She slept with them both.

Claire, Claire, I am suffering here. No one understands my transformation! Please answer me! 14. jan. 2018 kl. 11:49 skrev Yann Johansen <yjohansen@icloud.com>

She fell in love with Anouk. And yet, as far as she knows, she is not gay. Since, she has been married (twice) and has had a number of affairs with men; also she has had two children. Doesn't that count?

Where is Anouk now? she wonders. She has not thought of her in years—not quite true—in, more accurately, quite some time. Is Anouk, like Claire, a woman of a certain age, and living somewhere in France? On a farm, perhaps. An orderly and healthy life tending to her garden, to her cats (Claire remembers how, in Poona, dozens of feral cats roamed around, and how Anouk fed them). No doubt she has a husband—not Philippe, Claire ventures to guess—children, and grandchildren by now. Claire pictures Anouk, always trim and athletic—beautiful, really—bicycling on a country lane bordered by fields where red poppies grow in abundance.

At the time, she had written it as a sort of justification. After all, Rajneesh had offered and given her much—freedom, pleasure (not just sex), a feeling of community. Also, she had liked how he was against religion. Religion, he said, was a luxury and prayer just a plea. He was against politicians and priests, and that, too, had appealed to her.

I know you are reading this, Claire. You can't resist. You can't help yourself, you are addicted the same way people are addicted to cigarettes and to alcohol and to drugs—especially to drugs. 14. jan. 2018 kl. 12:06 skrev Yann Johansen <yjohansen@icloud.com>

But in Oregon, things changed. The atmosphere was no longer so joyful, so carefree, so friendly. No more singing and dancing. No more fucking. Instead there grew rivalries and resentments. And everyone had to work, often twelve hours a day. She painted rooms in the newly built houses—the same off-off-white color—and Anouk had to cook in the canteen. Everyone was tired. Also it snowed and no one was used to the cold. To make matters worse, Bhagwan decided not to speak for three years. His self-imposed silence was disturbing.

Eventually, Anouk and Philippe left. Philippe was the one who wanted to go. He had been put to work mixing cement and he kept saying, *"J'en ai marre,"* and Anouk, who wanted to stay, always answered him with *"Tu me fais chier."* Claire can still hear the tone of Anouk's voice and how she said it with such disdain. They argued a lot, but, in the end, Philippe won and they went back to France.

My name is Yon Yonson,
I live in Wisconsin.
I work in a lumber yard there.
The people I meet as
I walk down the street,
They say "Hello!"

Stop, Claire tells herself. The guy Yann is right. She is obsessive, or did he write "addicted"? Nearly the same thing.

Claire had stayed in Rajneeshpuram another six months, but it wasn't the same without Anouk and Philippe. Also, she, too, got sick. Not dysentery but some bronchial infection, on account of the paint fumes, she supposes. She coughed all the time.

She still coughs. "A smoker's cough," someone once told her, only she never smoked.

Not true.

She has smoked grass. She still does if the occasion presents itself.

Silence. No more emails from him. At least for now. She breathes a sigh of relief.

What time, she wonders, is it in Sweden now?

She googles: "time in Sweden."

7:15 P.M.

Maybe he is eating dinner.

She googles: "traditional Swedish dishes."

Pickled herring, lingonberries, potato pancakes, meatballs, crayfish . . .

She makes a face.

His emails have started up again.

Of course, she could turn off her computer and her phone. She could vacuum her apartment or read a book. Only she doesn't.

Why? she asks herself.

She is not sure she wants to think about her time with Rajneesh—over thirty years ago. Memories that have grown dim and uncertain. A bit like faded Polaroid photos—all but Anouk, who still remains fairly clear. Her red hair—not dyed, as it turned out. "A crown of fire" is how someone had once described it. But if she looks back and conjures up her own young self, she is unrecognizable.

How old is this Yann? Young, she guesses.

One day I will be famous. As famous as your Rajneesh. More famous. No one here understands that I am the real thing. 14. jan. 2018 kl. 12:17 skrev Yann Johansen <yjohansen@icloud.com>

Definitely crazy, she thinks. Or on drugs.

Do you remember how Rajneesh said that his body began to smell like jasmine? How he said the smell overpowered him? My body does not smell like jasmine or like a flower. It smells like cabbage and sweat and—but I don't want to offend you. Please answer me. 14. jan. 2018 kl. 12:20 skrev Yann Johansen <yjohansen@icloud.com>

In spite of herself, leaning down, she quickly sniffs at her underarm.

"Even after the Truth has been realized, there remains that strong, obstinate impression that one is still an ego—the agent and experiencer. This has to be carefully removed by living in a state of constant identification with the supreme non-dual Self. Full Awakening is the eventual ceasing of all the mental impressions of being an ego." 14. jan. 2018 kl. 12:23 skrev Yann Johansen <yjohansen@icloud.com>

More from Adi Shankara.

Adi Shankara was an eighth-century Hindu philosopher who preached self-realization.

What does "self-realization" really mean?

Fuck.

Anouk smelled good. She smelled of—she tries to think of what. Tea, maybe. The only time she had slept with a woman. At the time, it had felt like the most natural thing to do in the world; they had made each other come so easily.

Are you there, Claire? What are you thinking about? Are you thinking about fucking Bhagwan? Was it good? 14. jan. 2018 kl. 12:26 skrev Yann Johansen <yjohansen@icloud.com>

Claire feels herself blush. Is he a mind reader as well as a lunatic?

One time, out of the blue, Bhagwan had asked her to give him a pedicure. Claire had demurred—she told him she didn't know how. A test of some kind—he had insisted. A woman there had handed Claire the clippers.

"Be sure you don't draw any blood," the woman warned her.

With Bhagwan's feet on her lap, she had had to push back the cuticles and cut the tough yellow nails. Afterward, she had to massage the long, bony feet. The whole time she was in tears and could hardly see.

My name is Yon Yonson,
I live in Wisconsin.
I work in a lumber yard there.

Occasionally, when at night she cannot get to sleep, she counts the men she has slept with. She counts them in order of the worst lovers, then she reverses it and counts them in order of the best. The worst was a blind date—she has forgotten his name or more likely has blocked it out—a pilot who took her out in his small single-engine plane. They flew from Lake Tahoe Airport to San Francisco for dinner. On the way back, flying over the Sierra Nevadas, he complained that the radio navigation system he was using "did not know shit"—his words—and was sending him wrong signals. The sky was dark and cloud-covered; there were no visible stars. The snowcapped mountain peaks gleamed menacingly below them. At last they landed at the Lake Tahoe Airport, and afterward, relieved, Claire went to bed with the pilot. The pilot must have been relieved, too. Flying the plane, he had been chewing a stick of gum, and he kept the gum in his mouth while they fucked: *chomp, chomp,* next to her ear.

You really believe the Bhagwan was enlightened? Well, you are dead wrong. He was a manipulator, a charlatan, a crook, a hypocrite, an anti-Semite—I could go on and on listing his crimes. 14. jan. 2018 kl. 12:30 skrev Yann Johansen <yjohansen@icloud.com>

An anti-Semite? Claire shakes her head. The accusation had never occurred to her. The others, perhaps, yes, later in retrospect. He liked telling off-color jokes.

Have I frightened you, Claire? You are right to be frightened. Anything can happen. A meteor can fall from the sky or a huge tsunami can destroy the world. 14. jan. 2018 kl. 12:34 skrev Yann Johansen <yjohansen@icloud.com>

She had watched a tsunami video that showed entire houses, cars, boats, livestock, and people—people hanging on to debris and trying to remain afloat—being swept away and under anyway.

The other thing that Claire remembers about the video is how one commentator mentioned a herd of elephants on Sumatra. The elephants, he said, had very sensitive feet and, long before the wave hit the beach, they grew anxious and began to pace.

Rajneesh said silence was deafening and he was being drowned by the sound of a million bees. If that is not a statement by a crazy person I don't know what is. 14. jan. 2018 kl. 12:41 skrev Yann Johansen <yjohansen@icloud.com>

Perhaps she should answer and tell him to stop emailing her.

Better yet, just delete the emails.

Rajneesh was not a crazy person. He was a highly intelligent, ambitious, manipulative person. He claimed not to be enlightened; instead he said he was in "a natural state." His body functioned in an ideal way.

He wore flamboyant robes—a different one for each day—and had a long white beard and a piercing, hypnotic gaze. The rest of him, including his long, bony feet, Claire has made every effort to forget.

What, she wonders, does Yann look like? Thin and disheveled.

My name is Yon Yonson,
I live in Wisconsin.
I work in a lumber yard there.

All of a sudden, she feels sorry for him.

Not only am I bringing positive energy into the world, I am pure love. Trust me, Claire. 14. jan. 2018 kl. 12:46 skrev Yann Johansen <yjohansen@icloud.com>

Ah, love, Claire thinks. *That's what all the gurus say.* Bhagwan had once assured her of the same thing. At the time, foolishly, she had believed him.

"Shut the damn computer," she tells herself.

In bed that night, again sleepless and from habit, Claire reviews her list of lovers—good and bad. She does not include

Bhagwan on her list, nor, for that matter, does she include Anouk, although, just as she falls asleep, she remembers how Anouk had once confided to her that she had changed her name from Simone to Anouk, after Anouk Aimée the movie star. Anouk *Beloved.*

Acknowledgments

My thanks to Elisabeth Schmitz, Jazmine Goguen, Julia Berner-Tobin, Nancy Tan, Maureen Klier—attentive women all—and to Salvatore Destro.